JULIE ANDREWS'

Collection of Poems, Songs, and Lullabies

JULIE ANDREWS'

Collection of Poems, Songs, and Lullabies

Selected by
JULIE ANDREWS & EMMA WALTON HAMILTON
Paintings by JAMES McMULLAN

LITTLE, BROWN AND COMPANY
Books for Young Readers
New York   Boston

TABLE OF CONTENTS

★included on CD

SEA-FEVER

LAUGHING SONG

*included on CD

Introduction

So much of my life has been about music, which is perhaps why I'm always aware of the natural music in poetry. I'm also drawn to the words and meanings in a song, and I feel that many lyrics are poems in themselves. For me, it's so hard to separate the two that I chose to make this collection embrace both.

If you think about it, poems are the first things we learn and remember as children…

A, B, C, D, E, F, G—
H, I, J, K, L, M, N, O, P…

It rhymes, and has a certain rhythm and music to it—so it captures our ear.

Think about:

Twinkle, twinkle, little star,
How I wonder what you are?

or

Rain, rain, go away,
Come again another day!

Those early singsong poems begin the journey toward a love of poetry. I think of a poem as a gift, one that teaches us about the wonder of our world or captures a moment or a feeling that we may never have recognized until it was voiced for us.

Poems make us think. They make us feel or smile and understand more about ourselves. We look at the world a little differently after reading a poem, and we are the richer for it.

My father introduced me to poetry at a very young age. He loved to learn poems by heart and thought of them as beloved friends that he could call on whenever he needed. He bought me poetry books and read to me at bedtime, sharing his favorites—many of which are in this collection. Over the years, I've discovered my own favorites and passed them on to my children. I watch with pleasure as they now pass the tradition to my grandchildren.

I've tried my hand at writing poetry from time to time. It often helps to clarify the way I feel. In our family we write poems for each other as gifts, and because of its power to say exactly the right thing at the right time, we use poetry at important moments in our lives—celebrations, holidays, memorials, special events.

In our family we write poems for each other as gifts

Compiling this book has been a joy. My daughter Emma, with whom I co-author so many books in the Julie Andrews Collection, has been the perfect partner to bring our family favorites together. We have even discovered some new favorites. It shouldn't have come as a surprise (but it always did) when time and again we found that our choices were identical, and that the themes of nature, the arts, optimism, laughter, and respect for the world around us kept resurfacing.

This is a collection of our "favorite things"—and we hope that you find as much delight in these pages as we've experienced in putting them together.

All Things Bright and Beautiful

All Things Bright and Beautiful

used to sing "All Things Bright and Beautiful" at assembly in primary school. I didn't often have the chance to sing with other children, and I always got goose bumps when the entire student body raised its voice as one. It's such a beautiful and rousing hymn, and it seemed the perfect choice to start a section of poems and songs about nature in all its glory.

My father taught me to love nature as much as he did. A. E. Housman's "Loveliest of Trees" was his favorite poem (and it's probably mine—though that's like deciding which *song* I love best. I love so many, each for a different reason!). Dad and I would walk the English country lanes together in springtime, and he would point out the wonder of the blossoming cherry trees while sharing Housman's beautiful words. I have a large cherry tree in my own garden, which I cherish. Every spring I am reminded of the poem…and of Dad.

He believed that to see a miracle we need look no further than out our windows. Trees feed, nurture, clothe, and shelter us—they make the very air we breathe better, and they never ask for thanks. They endure extraordinary change and hardship, and even when a branch falls, it eventually feeds and replenishes the earth. It's both fun and awe-inspiring to guess the age of a majestic tree—and chances are it has witnessed and weathered more than we can ever imagine. I am so proud to include one of Dad's poems in this collection; not surprisingly, it's called "To an Oak Tree."

When I became a parent, I would take my children into the garden and we would play games of "discovery"—what colors,

To this day, Emma and I love poems and songs that make us taste, see, or feel the majesty of nature

even in the winter, could we spot? What sounds? What smells? To this day, Emma and I love poems and songs that make us taste, see, or feel the majesty of nature—the change of seasons, the power of weather—and we've included as many of them here as space would allow.

Julie Gold's "Every Living Thing" seems the perfect bookend for this section. Not only does it celebrate all things bright and beautiful, but it's a lovely call to action for us all to protect, preserve, and rejoice in the natural world.

—J. A.

All Things Bright and Beautiful (hymn)

All things bright and beautiful,
All creatures great and small,
All things wise and wonderful:
The Lord God made them all.

Each little flower that opens,
Each little bird that sings,
He made their glowing colors,
He made their tiny wings.

The purple-headed mountains,
The river running by,
The sunset and the morning
That brightens up the sky.

The cold wind in the winter,
The pleasant summer sun,
The ripe fruits in the garden,
He made them every one.

The tall trees in the greenwood,
The meadows where we play,
The rushes by the water,
To gather every day.

He gave us eyes to see them,
And lips that we might tell
How great is God Almighty,
Who has made all things well.

All things bright and beautiful,
All creatures great and small,
All things wise and wonderful:
The Lord God made them all.

Lyrics by Cecil Frances Alexander

Pied Beauty

Glory be to God for dappled things—
  For skies of couple-colour as a brinded cow;
    For rose-moles all in stipple upon trout that swim;
Fresh-firecoal chestnut-falls; finches' wings;
  Landscape plotted and pieced—fold, fallow, and plough;
  And all trades, their gear and tackle and trim.

All things counter, original, spare, strange;
  Whatever is fickle, freckled (who knows how?)
    With swift, slow; sweet, sour; adazzle, dim;
He fathers-forth whose beauty is past change:
        Praise him.

Gerard Manley Hopkins

Spring

Nature's bursting everywhere
Purple lilacs, perfumed air.
Geranium in searing reds,
Baby birds with fuzzy heads.
Sweep of green fields, flowers wild.
Blossoms falling, breezes mild.
Warming sunshine, gentle rain,
Laburnum's due to bloom again.
Giant cumulus aloft.
White, and seeming cotton soft.
Fir trees thrusting forth anew
Pale green tips and cones in view.
The whole imprinted on my mind
More than usual. So defined.
Such beauty and tranquility.
I wish it were contained in me.

Julie Andrews

These Precious Things

The forest glade so green and cool
Pine trees there on yonder hill
The lazy trout in sunlit pool
The summer night when all is still

The scent of roses in the breeze
The gentle humming of the bees
The woodland flowers so soft to touch
These precious things I love so much

I love to scorn the thought of gaining wealth
I want it not
I set no store by gold or rubies or pearls
I want them not

Simple things bring lasting happiness
Far more than these
Simple things
My heart will ever please

To saunter down a country lane
A stroll beside the moonlit sea
To see the fields of golden grain
The cattle grazing on the lea

To watch the newborn lambs at play
The fragrant scent of new-mown hay
The falling leaves at autumn's touch
These are the things
The precious things I love so much

Lyrics and music by
Howard Alexander and Billy Mayerl

April Rain Song

Let the rain kiss you.
Let the rain beat upon your head with silver liquid drops.
Let the rain sing you a lullaby.

The rain makes still pools on the sidewalk.
The rain makes running pools in the gutter.
The rain plays a little sleep-song on our roof at night—

And I love the rain.

Langston Hughes

Spring Rain

The storm came up so very quick,
   It couldn't have been quicker.
I should have brought my hat along,
   I should have brought my slicker.
My hair is wet, my feet are wet,
   I couldn't be much wetter.
I fell into a river once
   But this is even better.

Marchette Chute

Daffodils

I wandered lonely as a cloud
 That floats on high o'er vales and hills,
When all at once I saw a crowd,
 A host of golden daffodils
Beside the lake, beneath the trees,
Fluttering and dancing in the breeze.

Continuous as the stars that shine
 And twinkle on the Milky Way,
They stretched in never-ending line
 Along the margin of a bay:
Ten thousand saw I, at a glance,
Tossing their heads in sprightly dance.

The waves beside them danced, but they
 Outdid the sparkling waves in glee;
A poet could not but be gay,
 In such a jocund company;
I gazed—and gazed—but little thought
What wealth the show to me had brought.

For oft, when on my couch I lie,
 In vacant or in pensive mood,
They flash upon that inward eye
 Which is the bliss of solitude;
And then my heart with pleasure fills,
And dances with the daffodils.

William Wordsworth

Wildflowers

Wildflowers—I envy them.
They're brave.
Seeds cast by the wind to
land where they may,
they stay
and hold
against most hot, most cold.
They persevere, roots shallow
yet fierce and free.
They epitomize to me
all that I sometimes
yearn to be.

Julie Andrews

Trees

I think that I shall never see
A poem lovely as a tree.

A tree whose hungry mouth is prest
Against the earth's sweet flowing breast;

A tree that looks at God all day,
And lifts her leafy arms to pray;

A tree that may in summer wear
A nest of robins in her hair;

Upon whose bosom snow has lain;
Who intimately lives with rain.

Poems are made by fools like me,
But only God can make a tree.

Joyce Kilmer

Trees

Trees are the kindest things I know,
They do not harm, they simply grow

And spread a shade for sleepy cows,
And gather birds among their boughs.

They give us fruit in leaves above,
And wood to make our houses of,

And leaves to burn on Hallowe'en,
And in the Spring, new buds of green.

They are the first when day's begun
To touch the beams of morning sun,

They are the last to hold the light
When evening changes into night,

And when a moon floats on the sky
They hum a drowsy lullaby

Of sleepy children long ago . . .
Trees are the kindest things I know.

Harry Behn

Loveliest of Trees

Loveliest of trees, the cherry now
Is hung with bloom along the bough,
And stands about the woodland ride
Wearing white for Eastertide.

Now, of my threescore years and ten,
Twenty will not come again.
And take from seventy springs a score,
It only leaves me fifty more.

And since to look at things in bloom
Fifty springs are little room,
About the woodlands I will go
To see the cherry hung with snow.

A. E. Housman

To an Oak Tree

Three hundred changing summers, winters too,
Since first the quivering sapling struggled through,
A hundred thousand days since you were born,
And took to earth from out the green acorn.
Survived the pounding hoof and rooting pig,
Put out first fragile arms and then the big.

Two hundred years ago you firmly stood,
In promise rich as any in the wood,
Before your brothers in the claim to space,
With root and leaf creating your own place,
Had heard the thunder roar and breezes sing,
And from the storm given shelter to a king.

The next two hundred years had passed you by,
To find you yet fit neighbour to the sky,
And all man's need of ship, and church, and fire,
Had not assailed your own tremendous spire,
Which year by year from sap to solid core,
Unseen, unheard, took on a little more.

But nigh four thousand scintillating moons,
Three hundred Christmases, three hundred Junes
Have gone for nought and ever you must kneel
Before this artisan with bitter steel,
And to the sun and air lose acids raw,
Until the log is fit to meet the saw.

Till now beneath the softly-singing plane,
Your lustrous boards give up the secret grain,
And let the tiger-stripe medullar shine,
Across your straight and sturdy growing line,
And he who works with every shaving hears
How you grew into glory with the years.

And was it only Evolution's twist,
That man and timber came to co-exist,
Or did some greater mind regard that seed,
And plan it thus, so fit for every need?
Look at this chair, this door, that roof and know,
They could not be unless He meant it so.

E. C. Wells

Child's Song in Spring

The silver birch is a dainty lady,
   She wears a satin gown;
The elm tree makes the old churchyard shady,
   She will not live in town.

The English oak is a sturdy fellow,
   He gets his green coat late;
The willow is smart in a suit of yellow,
   While brown the beech trees wait.

Such a gay green gown God gives the larches—
   As green as He is good!
The hazels hold up their arms for arches
   When spring rides through the wood.

The chestnut's proud, and the lilac's pretty,
   The poplar's gentle and tall,
But the plane tree's kind to the poor dull city—
   I love him best of all!

Edith Nesbit

The Song of the Beech Tree Fairy

The trunks of Beeches are smooth and grey,
    Like tall straight pillars of stone
In great Cathedrals where people pray;
    Yet from tiny things they've grown.
About their roots is the moss; and wide
    Their branches spread, and high;
It seems to us, on the earth who bide,
    That their heads are in the sky.
And when Spring is here,
    and their leaves appear,
        With a silky fringe on each,
Nothing is seen so new and green
    As the new young green of Beech.
O the great grey Beech is young, is young,
    When, dangling soft and small,
Round balls of bloom from its twigs are hung,
    And the sun shines over all.

Cicely Mary Barker

27

Oh, What a Beautiful Mornin'!

There's a bright, golden haze on the meadow,
There's a bright, golden haze on the meadow.
The corn is as high as a elephant's eye,
An' it looks like it's climbin' clear up to the sky.

Oh, what a beautiful mornin'!
Oh, what a beautiful day!
I got a beautiful feelin'
Ev'rythin's goin' my way.

All the cattle are standin' like statues,
All the cattle are standin' like statues.
They don't turn their heads as they see me ride by,
But a little brown mav'rick is winkin' her eye.

Oh, what a beautiful mornin'!
Oh, what a beautiful day!
I got a beautiful feelin'
Ev'rythin's goin' my way.

All the sounds of the earth are like music—
All the sounds of the earth are like music.
The breeze is so busy, it don't miss a tree,
And a ol' weepin' willer is laughin' at me.

Oh, what a beautiful mornin'!
Oh, what a beautiful day!
I've got a beautiful feelin'
Ev'rythin's goin' my way…
Oh, what a beautiful day!

Lyrics and music by
Richard Rodgers and Oscar Hammerstein II

Lazy Afternoon

It's a lazy afternoon
    And the beetle bugs are zoomin
    And the tulip trees are bloomin
    And there's not another human
                    In view
                    But us two

It's a lazy afternoon
    And the farmer leaves his reapin
    In the meadow cows are sleepin
    And the speckled trouts stop leapin
                    Upstream
                    As we dream

A fat pink cloud hangs over the hill
    Unfolding like a rose
If you hold my hand and sit real still
    You can hear the grass as it grows

It's a lazy afternoon
    And I know a place that's quiet
    Cept for daisies running riot
    And there's no one passing by it
                    To see
Come spend this lazy afternoon with me.

Lyrics by John LaTouche
Music by Jerome Moross
(Abridged version)

Wind

This house has been far out at sea all night,
The woods crashing through darkness, the booming hills,
Winds stampeding the fields under the window
Floundering black astride and blinding wet

Till day rose; then under an orange sky
The hills had new places, and wind wielded
Blade-light, luminous and emerald,
Flexing like the lens of a mad eye.

At noon I scaled along the house-side as far as
The coal-house door. I dared once to look up—
Through the brunt wind that dented the balls of my eyes
The tent of the hills drummed and strained its guyrope,

The fields quivering, the skyline a grimace,
At any second to bang and vanish with a flap:
The wind flung a magpie away and a black-
Back gull bent like an iron bar slowly. The house

Rang like some fine green goblet in the note
That any second would shatter it. Now deep
In chairs, in front of the great fire, we grip
Our hearts and cannot entertain book, thought,

Or each other. We watch the fire blazing,
And feel the roots of the house move, but sit on,
Seeing the window tremble to come in,
Hearing the stones cry out under the horizons.

Ted Hughes

September

The breezes taste
   Of apple peel.
The air is full
   Of smells to feel—

Ripe fruit, old footballs,
   Drying grass,
New books and blackboard
   Chalk in class.

The bee, his hive
   Well-honeyed, hums
While Mother cuts
   Chrysanthemums.

Like plates washed clean
   With suds, the days
Are polished with
   A morning haze.

John Updike

Merry Autumn Days

'Tis pleasant on a fine spring morn
To see the buds expand;
'Tis pleasant in the summer time
To see the fruitful land;
'Tis pleasant on a winter's night
To sit around the blaze,
But what are joys like these, my boys,
To merry autumn days!

We hail the merry autumn days,
When leaves are turning red;
Because they're far more beautiful
Than anyone has said,
We hail the merry harvest time,
The gayest of the year;
The time of rich and bounteous crops,
Rejoicing and good cheer.

Charles Dickens

Autumn

The thistledown's flying, though the winds are all still,
On the green grass now lying, now mounting the hill,
The spring from the fountain now boils like a pot;
Through stones past the counting it bubbles red-hot.

The ground parched and cracked is like overbaked bread,
The greensward all wracked is, bents dried up and dead.
The fallow fields glitter like water indeed,
And gossamers twitter, flung from weed unto weed.

Hill-tops like hot iron glitter bright in the sun,
And the rivers we're eying burn to gold as they run;
Burning hot is the ground, liquid gold is the air;
Whoever looks round sees Eternity there.

John Clare

Something Told the Wild Geese

Something told the wild geese
   It was time to go.
Though the fields lay golden
   Something whispered,—"Snow."
Leaves were green and stirring,
   Berries, luster-glossed,
But beneath warm feathers
   Something cautioned,—"Frost."
All the sagging orchards
   Steamed with amber spice,
But each wild breast stiffened
   At remembered ice.
Something told the wild geese
   It was time to fly,—
Summer sun was on their wings,
   Winter in their cry.

Rachel Lyman Field

Smells

Through all the frozen winter
My nose has grown most lonely
For lovely, lovely, colored smells
That come in springtime only.

The purple smell of lilacs,
The yellow smell that blows
Across the air of meadows
Where bright forsythia grows.

The tall pink smell of peach trees,
The low white smell of clover,
And everywhere the great green smell
Of grass the whole world over.

Kathryn Worth

Every Living Thing

When I stand beneath the sky
And I watch the clouds roll by,
All at once I feel my spirit start to sing.
Suddenly, there are no words.
My soul's flying with the birds.
My heart's racing with the herds (and)
Every living thing.

When I stand beside a tree
And it gives its shade to me,
Everything I'd like to be, graceful and serene . . .
So much beauty to impart.
Sacred canvas, nature's art.
Every color.
Every part.
Every living thing.

Every bird and bee
Every chimpanzee
Creatures great and small.
Every daffodil
Every whippoorwill
I embrace them all.

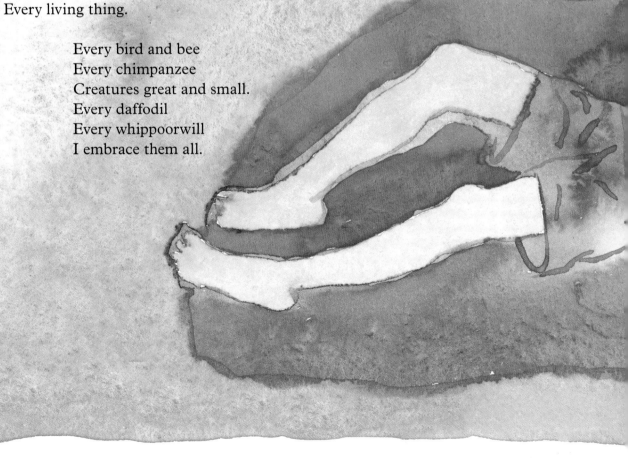

So I raise my single voice.
So I make my single choice.
To protect, preserve, rejoice (in)
Every living thing.

Every bird and bee
Every chimpanzee
Creatures great and small.
Every daffodil
Every whippoorwill
I embrace them all.

When I listen to my heart
I can always hear it sing.
Telling me that I am part (of)
Every living thing.

Lyrics and music by Julie Gold

Accentuate the Positive

Accentuate the Positive

 admit it. I *am* a "cockeyed optimist." My family teases me for my endless refrain, no matter how dubious the circumstances: "Are we lucky, or *what*?!"

Much to their annoyance, I suspect, I used to sing "Accentuate the Positive" to my kids. It's so original and witty…and it sticks. Somehow they always got the message better from those words than from anything I could have said myself.

If you think about it, "My Favorite Things"—which was such a joy for me to sing in the film *The Sound of Music* —has a similar message. Though actually a waltz with a beautiful melody, Oscar Hammerstein's lyric stands alone as a wonderful lesson in the power of positive thinking. Even when "the dog bites" or "the bee stings," we can still choose *how* we handle it.

Sometimes focusing on the positive can actually bring it about. Emma's poem "Faith" is a true story about her son, Sam. He was so convinced that he could invite a butterfly to land on him — and the miracle was that it

"*Are we lucky, or* what*?!*"

did. Emma says it helped remind her what grown-ups sometimes forget: that faith and optimism should never be overshadowed by skepticism.

I like to think of optimism as a muscle — to be stretched, flexed, encouraged. The more I use it, the happier I feel.

—*J. A.*

Accentuate the Positive

You've got to
Ac-cent-tchu-ate the positive
E-lim-my-nate the negative
Latch on to the affirmative
Don't mess with Mister In-Between

You've got to
Spread joy up to the maximum
Bring gloom down to the minimum
Have faith, or pandemonium's
Liable to walk upon the scene

To illustrate this last remark:
Jonah in the whale, Noah in the ark
What did they do
Just when everything looked so dark?

"Man," they said, "we better
Ac-cent-tchu-ate the positive
E-lim-my-nate the negative
Latch on to the affirmative
Don't mess with Mister In-Between!"

Lyrics by Johnny Mercer
Music by Harold Arlen
(Abridged version)

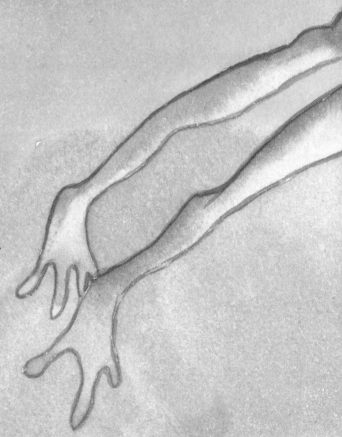

The Orange

At lunchtime I bought a huge orange—
The size of it made us all laugh.
I peeled it and shared it with Robert and Dave—
They got quarters and I had a half.

And that orange, it made me so happy,
As ordinary things often do
Just lately. The shopping. A walk in the park.
This is peace and contentment. It's new.

The rest of the day was quite easy.
I did all my jobs on my list
And enjoyed them and had some time over.
I love you. I'm glad I exist.

Wendy Cope

Sonnet 29

When, in disgrace with fortune and men's eyes,
I all alone beweep my outcast state
And trouble deaf heaven with my bootless cries
And look upon myself and curse my fate,
Wishing me like to one more rich in hope,
Featured like him, like him with friends possess'd,
Desiring this man's art and that man's scope,
With what I most enjoy contented least;
Yet in these thoughts myself almost despising,
Haply I think on thee and then my state,
Like to the lark at break of day arising
From sullen earth, sings hymns at heaven's gate;
For thy sweet love remember'd such wealth brings
That then I scorn to change my state with kings.

William Shakespeare

My Favorite Things

Raindrops on roses and whiskers on kittens,
Bright copper kettles and warm woolen mittens,
Brown paper packages tied up with strings—
These are a few of my favorite things.

Cream-colored ponies and crisp apple strudels,
Doorbells and sleigh-bells and schnitzel with noodles,
Wild geese that fly with the moon on their wings—
These are a few of my favorite things.

Girls in white dresses with blue satin sashes,
Snowflakes that stay on my nose and eyelashes,
Silver-white winters that melt into springs—
These are a few of my favorite things.

When the dog bites,
When the bee stings,
When I'm feeling sad,
I simply remember my favorite things
And then I don't feel so bad!

Lyrics and music by
Richard Rodgers and Oscar Hammerstein II

A Cockeyed Optimist

When the sky is a bright canary yellow
I forget ev'ry cloud I've ever seen—
So they call me a cockeyed optimist,
Immature and incurably green!

I have heard people rant and rave and bellow
That we're done and we might as well be dead—
But I'm only a cockeyed optimist,
And I can't get it into my head.

I hear the human race
Is falling on its face
And hasn't very far to go,
But ev'ry whippoorwill
Is selling me a bill
And telling me it just ain't so!

I could say life is just a bowl of Jell-O
And appear more intelligent and smart,
But I'm stuck, like a dope,
With a thing called hope,
And I can't get it out of my heart!
Not this heart.

Lyrics and music by
Richard Rodgers and Oscar Hammerstein II

The Optimist

The optimist fell ten stories,
   And at each window bar
He shouted to the folks inside:
   "Doing all right so far!"

               Anonymous

Certainty

I never saw a moor,
I never saw the sea;
Yet know I how the heather looks,
And what a wave must be.

I never spoke with God,
Nor visited in Heaven;
Yet certain am I of the spot
As if the chart were given.

            Emily Dickinson

Dust of Snow

The way a crow
Shook down on me
The dust of snow
From a hemlock tree

Has given my heart
A change of mood
And saved some part
Of a day I had rued.

Robert Frost

Be Like the Bird

Be like the bird, who
Resting in his flight
On a twig too slight
Feels it give way beneath him,
Yet sings
Knowing he has wings.

Victor Hugo

Faith

You said to us, your arms outstretched
—a golden boy of three,
"I'm waiting for a butterfly
to come and land on me."

Your dad and I were worried.
We exchanged a little smile.
"You know," Dad offered tenderly,
"that might take a while."

"Try again," I added,
"when the bushes are in flower…"
But still you stood there, motionless,
for what seemed like an hour.

"How about a game of catch?"
Dad hoped he could distract.
"*After* the butterfly," you said,
with confidence and tact.

We knew, as grown-ups do, of course,
this dream could not come true—
that tears and disappointment
would undoubtedly ensue.

Yet suddenly, from nowhere,
just the way you had foretold,
Her Majesty appeared
and settled lightly on your shoulder.

Your smile extended ear to ear.
You looked at Dad and me.
She flexed her lovely orange wings,
and you said, simply, "See?"

Emma Walton Hamilton

Hold Fast Your Dreams

Hold fast your dreams!
Within your heart
Keep one still, secret spot
Where dreams may go,
And, sheltered so,
May thrive and grow
Where doubt and fear are not.
O keep a place apart,
Within your heart,
For little dreams to go!

Think still of lovely things that are not true.
Let wish and magic work at will in you.
Be sometimes blind to sorrow. Make believe!
Forget the calm that lies
In disillusioned eyes.
Though we all know that we must die,
Yet you and I
May walk like gods and be
Even now at home in immortality.

We see so many ugly things—
Deceits and wrongs and quarrelings;
We know, alas! we know
How quickly fade
The color in the west,
The bloom upon the flower,
The bloom upon the breast
And youth's blind hour.
Yet keep within your heart
A place apart
Where little dreams may go,
May thrive and grow.
Hold fast—hold fast your dreams!

Louise Driscoll

51

You Must Believe in Spring

When lonely feelings chill
The meadows of your mind,
Just think if Winter comes,
Can Spring be far behind?

Beneath the deepest snows,
The secret of a rose
Is merely that it knows
You must believe in Spring!

Just as a tree is sure
Its leaves will reappear;
It knows its emptiness
Is just the time of year.

The frozen mountain dreams
Of April's melting streams,
How crystal clear it seems,
You must believe in Spring!

You must believe in love
And trust it's on its way,
Just as the sleeping rose
Awaits the kiss of May.

So in a world of snow,
Of things that come and go,
Where what you think you know,
You can't be certain of,
You must believe in Spring and love.

Lyrics by Alan and Marilyn Bergman
Music by Michael Legrand

Growing Up

Growing Up

We couldn't do a collection of poems for the family without celebrating childhood itself — and who does it better than A. A. Milne? "Rice Pudding" is exactly the way I used to feel about spinach — happily I've grown to love it!

"The Secrets of Our Garden" reminds me so much of my own childhood — the hours I spent riding my makeshift hobby horses made from beanpoles, pretending our tiny orchard was a fruit shop, delighting in warm raspberries or gooseberries, finding my own secret hiding place in the forsythia bush, inhaling the perfume of the lilacs, sweet peas, and lilies of the valley.

Emma and I challenged each other to write a poem about parenthood. Typically, we both chose the same subject — daughters.

"Our Lady of Perpetual Demand" is about Emma's daughter, Hope. In a family where the women, though strong, tend to put everyone else's needs before their own, it's refreshing that the littlest one already knows *exactly* who she is and what she wants, and isn't afraid to say it!

I wrote "Observation" about Emma herself. Though only nine years old, her conviction that womanhood was proceeding according to plan was enchanting, despite the fact that there was absolutely *no* evidence to support it at that moment.

We all wish for our children
the best life has to offer

Perhaps nothing expresses parenthood, and the tidal wave of love we feel for our children, more warmly than Frank Loesser's "More I Cannot Wish You." We all wish for our children the best life has to offer, but perhaps our deepest desire is that they might one day find and experience a love as great as ours is for them.

—*J. A.*

Growing Up

My father and I climbed the hill . . .
We didn't go the easy way.
We didn't take the tourists' path
that sunny, summer's day.

We slowly climbed through shale and sand,
shrubs and grassy knolls.
I scraped my knees on jagged stones
and clung to crumbling walls.

I grumbled, sweated, cried from thirst,
knelt at a stream and drank my fill.
Compared to my pulsing, raging heart,
the water seemed quite calm and still.

We finally scrambled to the peak,
Dad hiking me by collared shirt.
The view was just magnificent.
My legs were jelly. My shoes hurt.

At the time I felt just miserable.
"Therapeutic!" said my dad.
He was right, of course. In retrospect
it was a great day to have had.

Julie Andrews

On My Way

Looking out at the world I see
So many dreams, so many possibilities
Climbing a mountain
or maybe a tree
Life is calling to me

Well, I'm on my way
I'm on my way

Though my journey has only begun
I'll keep growing, won't ever be done
Finding my way from a walk to a run
Reaching up for the sun

Well, I'm on my way
I'm on my way

And if I should stumble
Or if I do some foolish things
Hold me close, then let me fly
Give me roots and wings

'Cause I'm on my way
I'm on my way

Lyrics by Emma Walton Hamilton,
Lisa Michaelis, and Billy Schlosser
Music by Billy Schlosser and Lisa Michaelis

Home! You're Where It's Warm Inside

Home! You are a special place;
you're where I wake and wash my face,
brush my teeth and comb my hair,
change my socks and underwear,
clean my ears and blow my nose,
try on all my parents' clothes.

Home! You're where it's warm inside,
where my tears are gently dried,
where I'm comforted and fed,
where I'm forced to go to bed,
where there's always love to spare;
Home! I'm glad that you are there.

Jack Prelutsky

The Secrets of Our Garden

People think it's only a garden,
    With roses along the wall;
I'll tell you the truth about it—
    It isn't a garden at all!

It's really Robin Hood's forest,
    And over by that big tree
Is the very place where fat Friar Tuck
    Fought with the Miller of Dee.

And back of the barn is the cavern
    Where Rob Roy really hid;
On the other side is a treasure-chest
That belonged to Captain Kidd.

That isn't a pond you see there,
    It's an ocean deep and wide,
Where six-masted ships are waiting
    To sail on the rising tide.

Of course it looks like a garden,
    It's all so sunny and clear—
You'd be surprised if you really knew
    The things that have happened here!

Rupert Sargent Holland
Adapted by James W. King

61

My Shadow

I have a little shadow that goes in and out with me,
And what can be the use of him is more than I can see.
He is very, very like me from the heels up to the head;
And I see him jump before me, when I jump into my bed.

The funniest thing about him is the way he likes to grow—
Not at all like proper children, which is always very slow;
For he sometimes shoots up taller like an india-rubber ball,
And he sometimes gets so little that there's none of him at all.

He hasn't got a notion of how children ought to play,
And can only make a fool of me in every sort of way.
He stays so close behind me, he's a coward you can see;
I'd think shame to stick to nursie as that shadow sticks to me!

One morning, very early, before the sun was up,
I rose and found the shining dew on every buttercup;
But my lazy little shadow, like an arrant sleepy-head,
Had stayed at home behind me and was fast asleep in bed.

Robert Louis Stevenson

Rice Pudding

What is the matter with Mary Jane?
She's crying with all her might and main,
And she won't eat her dinner—rice pudding again—
What *is* the matter with Mary Jane?

What is the matter with Mary Jane?
I've promised her dolls and a daisy-chain,
And a book about animals—all in vain—
What *is* the matter with Mary Jane?

What is the matter with Mary Jane?
She's perfectly well, and she hasn't a pain;
But, look at her, now she's beginning again!—
What *is* the matter with Mary Jane?

What is the matter with Mary Jane?
I've promised her sweets and a ride in the train,
And I've begged her to stop for a bit and explain—
What *is* the matter with Mary Jane?

What is the matter with Mary Jane?
She's perfectly well and she hasn't a pain,
And it's lovely rice pudding for dinner again!
What *is* the matter with Mary Jane?

A. A. Milne

Our Lady of Perpetual Demand

I want, I want, I want!
You say,
When can I have it? *When?*
Another day it's
No! I won't!
And no, no, NO! again.
I sigh.
I ask for manners,
Counter "I don't want to hear it!"
But in my heart I celebrate
Your dazzling strength of spirit.

Emma Walton Hamilton

Observation

Sweet, beloved daughter of mine . . .
I recall when you were merely nine.
I passed your room one sunny day
and saw you, caught in the mirror's sway.

You happily turned this way and that,
and cupped your chest
(which was seriously flat).
In profile, you murmured the priceless line,
"Ha!" you said.
"Coming along just fine."

Julie Andrews

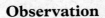

65

I Did Not Eat Your Ice Cream

I did not eat your ice cream,
I did not swipe your socks,
I did not stuff your lunch box
with rubber bands and rocks.

I did not hide your sweater,
I did not dent your bike,
it must have been my sister,
we look a lot alike.

Jack Prelutsky

Sick

"I cannot go to school today,"
Said little Peggy Ann McKay.
"I have the measles and the mumps,
A gash, a rash and purple bumps.
My mouth is wet, my throat is dry,
I'm going blind in my right eye.
My tonsils are as big as rocks,
I've counted sixteen chicken pox
And there's one more—that's seventeen,
And don't you think my face looks green?
My leg is cut, my eyes are blue—
It might be instamatic flu.
I cough and sneeze and gasp and choke,
I'm sure that my left leg is broke—
My hip hurts when I move my chin,
My belly button's caving in,
My back is wrenched, my ankle's sprained,
My 'pendix pains each time it rains.
My nose is cold, my toes are numb,
I have a sliver in my thumb.
My neck is stiff, my voice is weak,
I hardly whisper when I speak.
My tongue is filling up my mouth,
I think my hair is falling out.
My elbow's bent, my spine ain't straight,
My temperature is one-o-eight.
My brain is shrunk, I cannot hear,
There is a hole inside my ear.
I have a hangnail, and my heart is—what?
What's that? What's that you say?
You say today is . . . Saturday?
G'bye, I'm going out to play!"

Shel Silverstein

More I Cannot Wish You

Velvet I can wish you
For the collar of your coat
And fortune smiling all along your way
But more I cannot wish you
Than to wish you find your love
Your own true love, this day
Mansions I can wish you
Seven footmen all in red
And calling cards upon a silver tray
But more I cannot wish you
Than to wish you find your love
Your own true love, this day
Standing there
Gazing at you
Full of the bloom of youth
Standing there
Gazing at you
With the sheep's eye
And the lickerish tooth
Music I can wish you
Merry music while you're young
And wisdom when your hair has turned to gray
But more I cannot wish you
Than to wish you find your love
Your own true love, this day
With the sheep's eye
And the lickerish tooth
And the strong arms to carry you away

Lyrics and music by Frank Loesser

Bedtime Blessing

Bedtime Blessing

iven that we spend a third of our lives in bed, it follows that bedtime — with its challenges as well as comforts — is a subject worth including.

I've always believed that the moments before sleep are among the most important of the day. Tucking my kids in at night with stories, lullabies, and feelings of safety and contentment probably nurtured me as much as it did them. I hope it had the power to sweeten their dreams.

Emma reads stories and Henry Johnstone's "Goodnight Prayer" with her children every night before bed. Books are stacked, strewn, and stored *everywhere* in her house — on the side tables, in the bathroom, by the bed, in the kitchen — ready for *any* opportunity to indulge in family reading time.

One of my personal favorites in this section is "The Trick" by John Mole. Sometimes I have a hard time falling asleep, and this poem offers a wonderful alternative to counting sheep. When I start to toss and turn, it helps to conjure up a favorite image or place, real or imagined— and next thing I know, it's morning.

Lullabies, of course, are a time-honored way to invite sleep. "Rock-a-bye Baby" never worked for me, given its

I've always believed that the moments before sleep are among the most important of the day.

abrupt and rather disturbing conclusion. Songs that soothe are more my cup of tea. Although Stephen Sondheim's "Not While I'm Around" and Alan and Marilyn Bergman's "And I'll Be There" were not perhaps intended as such, they seem to me to be perfect lullabies, for while they touch on the fears that often arise in the dark, they quickly dispel them with words of love and safety.

—J. A.

Bedtime Blessing

Bedtime.
Curling up,
Finding a poem or two.

Reading.
Snuggling down,
Sharing the wonder with you.

Listen, ponder,
Feel the release.
Imagine, wonder,
Surrender to peace.

Everything warm and cozy
As you drift towards dreamland.
Wake the next day with grace in your heart
And hold the world in your hand.

Night

The sun descending in the west,
   The evening star does shine;
The birds are silent in their nest,
   And I must seek for mine.
The moon, like a flower,
In heaven's high bower,
With silent delight
Sits and smiles on the night.

Farewell, green fields and happy groves,
   Where flocks have took delight.
Where lambs have nibbled, silent moves
   The feet of angels bright;
Unseen they pour blessing,
And joy without ceasing,
On each bud and blossom,
And each sleeping bosom.

William Blake
(Abridged version)

Vespers

Little Boy kneels at the foot of the bed,
Droops on the little hands little gold head.
Hush! Hush! Whisper who dares!
Christopher Robin is saying his prayers.

God bless Mummy. I know that's right.
Wasn't it fun in the bath tonight?
The cold's so cold, and the hot's so hot.
Oh! *God bless Daddy*—I quite forgot.

If I open my fingers a little bit more,
I can see Nanny's dressing-gown on the door.
It's a beautiful blue, but it hasn't a hood.
Oh! *God bless Nanny and make her good.*

Mine has a hood, and I lie in bed,
And pull the hood right over my head,
And I shut my eyes, and I curl up small,
And nobody knows that I'm there at all.

Oh! *Thank you, God, for a lovely day.*
And what was the other I had to say?
I said "Bless Daddy," so what can it be?
Oh! Now I remember. *God bless Me.*

Little Boy kneels at the foot of the bed,
Droops on the little hands little gold head.
Hush! Hush! Whisper who dares!
Christopher Robin is saying his prayers.

A. A. Milne

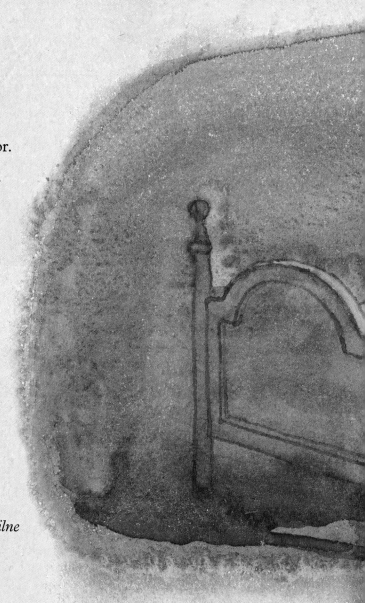

Not While I'm Around

Nothing's gonna harm you,
not while I'm around.
Nothing's gonna harm you, no sir,
not while I'm around.
Demons are prowling
ev'rywhere nowadays.
I'll send them howling,
I don't care, I've got ways.

No-one's gonna hurt you,
no-one's gonna dare.
Others can desert you,
Not to worry; whistle, I'll be there.
Demons'll charm you with a smile
for a while, but in time,
nothing can harm you,
not while I'm around.

Lyrics and music by Stephen Sondheim
(Abridged version)

Good Night Prayer

Father, unto Thee I pray,
Thou hast guarded me all day;
Safe I am while in thy sight,
Safely let me sleep tonight.

Bless my friends, the whole world bless;
Help me to learn helpfulness;
Keep me ever in Thy sight;
So to all I say goodnight.

Henry Johnstone

77

My Bed Is a Boat

My bed is like a little boat;
    Nurse helps me in when I embark;
She girds me in my sailor's coat
    And starts me in the dark.

At night, I go on board and say
    Good-night to all my friends on shore;
I shut my eyes and sail away
    And see and hear no more.

And sometimes things to bed I take,
    As prudent sailors have to do;
Perhaps a slice of wedding-cake,
    Perhaps a toy or two.

All night across the dark we steer;
    But when the day returns at last,
Safe in my room, beside the pier,
    I find my vessel fast.

Robert Louis Stevenson

Sweet Dreams

I wonder as into bed I creep
What it feels like to fall asleep.
I've told myself stories, I've counted sheep,
But I'm always asleep when I fall asleep.
Tonight my eyes I will open keep,
And I'll stay awake till I fall asleep,
Then I'll know what it feels like to fall asleep,
Asleep,
Asleeep,
Asleeeep . . .

Ogden Nash

Wynken, Blynken, and Nod (Dutch lullaby)

Wynken, Blynken, and Nod one night
   Sailed off in a wooden shoe—
Sailed on a river of crystal light,
   Into a sea of dew.
"Where are you going, and what do you wish?"
   The old moon asked the three.
"We have come to fish for the herring fish
   That live in this beautiful sea;
   Nets of silver and gold have we!"
        Said Wynken,
        Blynken,
        And Nod.

The old moon laughed and sang a song,
   As they rocked in the wooden shoe,
And the wind that sped them all night long
   Ruffled the waves of dew.
The little stars were the herring fish
   That lived in that beautiful sea—
"Now cast your nets wherever you wish—
   Never afeard are we";
   So cried the stars to the fishermen three:
        Wynken,
        Blynken,
        And Nod.

All night long their nets they threw
   To the stars in the twinkling foam—
Then down from the skies came the wooden shoe,
   Bringing the fishermen home;
'Twas all so pretty a sail it seemed
   As if it could not be,
And some folks thought 'twas a dream they'd dreamed
   Of sailing that beautiful sea—
   But I shall name you the fishermen three:
        Wynken,
        Blynken,
        And Nod.

Wynken and Blynken are two little eyes,
   And Nod is a little head,
And the wooden shoe that sailed the skies
   Is a wee one's trundle-bed.
So shut your eyes while mother sings
   Of wonderful sights that be,
And you shall see the beautiful things
   As you rock in the misty sea,
   Where the old shoe rocked the fishermen three:
        Wynken,
        Blynken,
        And Nod.

Eugene Field

Bed Mate

Whenever lightning strikes at night
    And thunder starts to boom,
My little sister, Ann Marie,
    Comes creeping to my room.

I don't mind moving over
    So there's room for Ann Marie,
I just wish that she would not put
    Her cold feet next to me!

Constance Andrea Keremes

Genius

"Sis! Wake up!" I whisper
in the middle of the night.

    Urgently, I shake her
    till she switches on the light.

The spiral notebook in my hand
provides her quick relief.

    It tells her there's no danger
    of a break-in by a thief.

"Okay," she says, then props herself
up vertically in bed.

    She nods for me to read my work.
    I cough, then forge ahead.

The last verse of my poem leaves
her silent as a mouse.

    I worry till she says, "We have
    a genius in the house."

Nikki Grimes

The Trick

One night, when I couldn't sleep,
My dad said
Think of the tomatoes in the greenhouse

And I did.
It wasn't the same as counting sheep
Or anything like that.

It was just not being in my room forever
On a hot bed
Restless, turning and turning,

But out there, with the patient gaze of moonlight
Blessing each ripe skin
And our old zinc watering-can with its sprinkler,

Shining through a clear glass pane
Which slowly clouded over into
Drowsy, comfortable darkness

Till I woke and came downstairs to breakfast
Saying *Thank you, Dad,*
I thought of them. It did the trick.

John Mole

And I'll Be There

I'll be there with you
Whenever the world seems far too wide,
Though you may not always see me,
I'm right there by your side.
When you're frightened and pull up the covers,
Though it's only a creaky stair.
If the rainbows fade,
Don't you be afraid,
For I promise you I'll be there.

When the shadows come and moonlight
Paints pictures on the wall,
And you're feeling lost and lonely,
Like no one cares at all.
When you can't chase the demons inside you,
And it's more than a soul can bear,
You must never fear,
They will disappear,
Look around you and I'll be there.

There'll be times when friends desert you
And life may let you down,
And those moments leave you feeling
Like the circus just left town.
You just tell me if anything hurts you—
I'll make it alright—I swear!
Sure as rainbows bend,
My forever friend,
I can promise you I'll be there.

A kiss and a smile,
Then dream for a while,
You'll wake up and I'll be there!

Lyrics by Alan and Marilyn Bergman
Music by Dave Grusin

Talk to the Animals

Talk to the Animals

Emma and I are both animal lovers, and between us our households have been home to a motley assortment of cats, dogs, hamsters, canaries, guinea pigs, turtles, a Bearded Dragon lizard, dozens of fish, and a host of strays and unsolicited visitors—as well as the rabbits, chipmunks, raccoons, possums, squirrels, seagulls, songbirds, and deer that populate our backyards!

I used to sing "The Wren" when I was a child performer in the music halls. One of nature's smallest birds, the shy little wren has a perky, upright tail no bigger than half my thumb, and a voice that won't quit. As a singer, I find it amazing that this tiny creature can make such a big and joyful sound. I am thrilled when a wren comes to visit my garden.

"Adelie Penguin" was written by Emma's father, Tony Walton. For reasons that remain a mystery, he is *crazy* about penguins and has a collection of carved, stuffed, ceramic, and toy versions of the quirky little birds to rival the number in the Antarctic. We chose to include Tony's poem not just for personal reasons, or because it's fun, but because it so cleverly reminds us of the value of diversity.

My grandfather was the manager of a coal mine in the north of England and was known in his village as "The Pitman's Poet." He sold his poems door-to-door, and performed them at local parties and concert halls. Back then, before mining was mechanized, small ponies were used "down pit" to haul the wagons of coal to the mine

As a singer, I find it amazing that this tiny creature can make such a big and joyful sound.

shaft. They seldom saw the light of day but were strong, stouthearted, patient, and loyal to their "drivers." I only recently discovered Grandfather Morris's "A Pit Pony's Memory of the Strike," and I'm so pleased to introduce it here.

I loved ponies when I was a child and longed for one of my own — so I *had* to include Robert Frost's "The Runaway." I always wished, when I read the words "Whose colt?" I could have shouted out, "He's *mine*!"

—*J. A.*

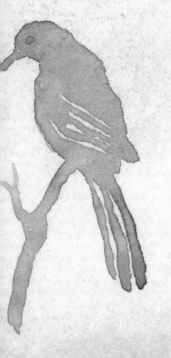

Talk to the Animals

If we could talk to the animals, just imagine it
Chatting to a chimp in chimpanzee
Imagine talking to a tiger, chatting to a cheetah
What a neat achievement that would be.

If we could talk to the animals, learn their languages
Maybe take an animal degree.
We'd study elephant and eagle, buffalo and beagle,
Alligator, guinea pig, and flea.

We would converse in polar bear and python,
And we could curse in fluent kangaroo.
If people asked us, can you speak in rhinoceros,
We'd say, "Of courserous, can't you?"

If we could talk to the animals, learn their languages
Think of all the things we could discuss
If we could walk with the animals, talk with the animals,
Grunt and squeak and squawk with the animals,
And they could squeak and squawk and speak and talk to us.

Lyrics and music by
Leslie Bricusse

Feed the Birds

Early each day to the steps of Saint Paul's
The little old bird woman comes.
In her own special way to the people she calls,
"Come, buy my bags full of crumbs.

Come feed the little birds, show them you care
And you'll be glad if you do.
Their young ones are hungry,
Their nests are so bare;
All it takes is tuppence from you."

Feed the birds, tuppence a bag,
Tuppence, tuppence, tuppence a bag.
"Feed the birds," that's what she cries,
While overhead, her birds fill the skies.

All around the cathedral the saints and apostles
Look down as she sells her wares.
Although you can't see it, you know they are smiling
Each time someone shows that he cares.

Though her words are simple and few,
Listen, listen, she's calling to you:
"Feed the birds, tuppence a bag,
Tuppence, tuppence, tuppence a bag."

Lyrics and music by
Richard M. Sherman and Robert B. Sherman

The Wren

A wren just under my window
  Has suddenly, sweetly sung;
He woke me from my slumbers
  With his shrill, sweet tongue.

It was so very early,
  The dewdrops were not dry,
And pearly cloudlets floated
  Across the rosy sky.

His nest is in the ivy
  Where his little wife sits all day,
And by her side he sings to her,
  And never flies far away.

Lyrics by A.S.
Music by Liza Lehmann

Duck's Ditty

All along the backwater,
Through the rushes tall,
Ducks are a-dabbling,
Up tails all!

Ducks' tails, drakes' tails,
Yellow feet a-quiver,
Yellow bills all out of sight
Busy in the river!

Slushy green undergrowth
Where the roach swim—
Here we keep our larder,
Cool and full and dim.

Every one for what he likes!
We like to be
Heads down, tails up,
Dabbling free!

High in the blue above
Swifts whirl and call—
We are down a-dabbling
Up tails all!

Kenneth Grahame
From A Wind in the Willows

Adelie Penguin

Adelie Penguin
Has dozens of cousins
Who live in the large penguin pool at the zoo.
They all look alike
So they all have the problem
Of trying to figure out which one is who.

The thing with their name on
That came on their crates with them
Somehow was lost when the last of them came.
Now all of them seem
So extremely identical
None of them knows just who goes with which name.

Yesterday Adelie
Wanted to clarify
All of the muddle she had in her head.
Unable to label
Her nearest and dearest
She pondered and puzzled and here's what she said:

"Phooey and fishbubbles!
Drat and darnation!
Why *does* each relation seem somehow the same one?
This bothers me badly,"
Said Adelie sadly
And cried as she tried to decide how to name one.

"Perhaps if a penguin
Could dress like a person—
Then which one was which would be easy to tell.
You could guess who was who
By the clothes that we chose.
But what could we wear that would fit on us well?

"We couldn't wear trousers
Nor even nice underthings.
It's probably best just to settle for shirts
With lovely large lettering
Showing distinctly
That this shirt is Susie's or that shirt is Bert's.

"Top hats with our names on
Might help with the problem,
And look rather smart with our shiny tail coats.
But how could we see
When out diving and swimming?
We'd just have to do all our travel in boats.

"There *must* be a somewhat
More civilized system
If only we somehow could start to employ one.
Perhaps I should line up
Each penguin and list them
According to which is a girl or a boy one.

(continued)

95

"The big ones are boy ones,
The girls are more delicate.
Shy ones are females while boy ones are bold."
(These were all things you see
Deep in her memory
Things she had read about
Things she'd been told.)

"Girls are obedient
Boys are more mischievous
Most boys are muscular—females are frail.
Girls are more sensitive
Boys are more coarse, of course.
The ones with big flippers are certainly male."

All of this rigmarole
Adelie sang aloud
While she arranged her relations by sex—
Some she was right about,
Most she got badly wrong!
Still she sang as she hung all their names round their necks:

"This must be Susie
Susies are sensible
Sane and responsible—Myrtles are meek.
This must be Maisie
For Maisies are lazy
But proud of the pretty pink bump on their beak.

"Bertie and Spike
Are alike in their cheekiness—
Boys are *all* cheerfully cheeky you see.
Charlie's a chatterbox
Maisie's a lazy lox—
Which one is Adelie?
Mercy! That's me."

Oh that our Adelie
Could have been born today
Knowing that most of that claptrap's all wrong—
We are not Tinkertoys
Very few girls and boys
Fit into formulas found in a song.

Most of our make-ups
Are magical riddles—
Muddled up mixtures
Of shadow and light
For we are all born
With so many fine shadings
Not even a *penguin*
Is *just* black and white.

Tony Walton

97

The Cow

The friendly cow all red and white,
  I love with all my heart:
She gives me cream with all her might,
  To eat with apple-tart.

She wanders lowing here and there,
  And yet she cannot stray,
All in the pleasant open air,
  The pleasant light of day;

And blown by all the winds that pass
  And wet with all the showers,
She walks among the meadow grass
  And eats the meadow flowers.

Robert Louis Stevenson

The Runaway

Once when the snow of the year was beginning to fall,
We stopped by a mountain pasture to say, "Whose colt?"
A little Morgan had one forefoot on the wall,
The other curled at his breast. He dipped his head
And snorted at us. And then he had to bolt.
We heard the miniature thunder where he fled,
And we saw him, or thought we saw him, dim and grey,
Like a shadow against the curtain of falling flakes.
"I think the little fellow's afraid of the snow.
He isn't winter-broken. It isn't play
With the little fellow at all. He's running away.
I doubt if even his mother could tell him, 'Sakes,
It's only weather.' He'd think she didn't know!
Where is his mother? He can't be out alone."
And now he comes again with a clatter of stone
And mounts the wall again with whited eyes
And all his tail that isn't hair up straight.
He shudders his coat as if to throw off flies.
"Whoever it is that leaves him out so late,
When other creatures have gone to stall and bin,
Ought to be told to come and take him in."

Robert Frost

99

Nicholas Nye

Thistle and darnel and dock grew there,
   And a bush, in the corner, of may,
On the orchard wall I used to sprawl
   In the blazing heat of the day;
Half asleep and half awake,
   While the birds went twittering by,
And nobody there my lone to share
   But Nicholas Nye.

Nicholas Nye was lean and grey,
   Lame of leg and old,
More than a score of donkey's years
   He had been since he was foaled;
He munched the thistles, purple and spiked,
   Would sometimes stoop and sigh,
And turn to his head, as if he said,
   "Poor Nicholas Nye!"

Alone with his shadow he'd drowse in the meadow,
   Lazily swinging his tail,
At break of day he used to bray—
   Not much too hearty and hale;
But a wonderful gumption was under his skin,
   And a clean calm light in his eye.
And once in a while; he'd smile—
   Would Nicholas Nye.

Seem to be smiling at me, he would,
　From his bush, in the corner, of may—
Bony and ownerless, widowed and worn,
　Knobble-kneed, lonely and grey;
And over the grass would seem to pass
　'Neath the deep dark blue of the sky,
Something much better than words between me
　And Nicholas Nye.

But dusk would come in the apple boughs,
　The green of the glow-worm shine,
The birds in nest would crouch to rest,
　And home I'd trudge to mine;
And there, in the moonlight, dark with dew,
　Asking not wherefore nor why,
Would brood like a ghost, and as still as a post,
　Old Nicholas Nye.

Walter de la Mare

A Pit Pony's Memory of the Strike

I'm only a pit pony and where I prove my worth,
Is where there is no daylight—in the bowels of the earth.
But one day, I can tell you, I was filled with joy untold . . .
They took me to pit bottom and my eyes they did blindfold.
In the cage,[1] then up the shaft, I seemed to go with pride,
The winder[2] must have thought of me, 'twas such a gentle ride;
At last I'm on the surface, from the cage I'm led away.
They take the cover off my eyes; I see the light of day!

Later on, my mates came up—and then it came to pass
They took us down into a field and turned us out to grass.
We held a meeting in that field; 'twas just beside a dyke,[3]
And we came to the conclusion that the pit must be on strike.

We thought of "Hodges" and "Herbert Smith," and then my mate called Guss
Sang, "They are jolly good fellows and so say all of us."
Then as we jazzed around that field, each pony thought that day
That he had found the Happy Land, far, far away.

One day our boss he came, you know, and made us feel forlorn.
We thought that we were going back where the "moggies"[4] pinch our corn.
To our delight he took us amongst crowds and smiling faces.
Alas! This was our jubilee[5]—the first Pit Pony Races.
Now first I heard a tremendous noise, which made the people shift;
I said to myself, "There must be a runner[6] down the drift."[7]
But as the noise grew nearer, 'twas music—understand?
I fancied I was "Kissing Cup" as I marched behind the band.

(continued)

---

1 In a mine shaft, the cage, similar to an elevator car, is used for hoisting personnel and materials.
2 The person in charge of winding the winch to hoist the cage up and down
3 Either a ditch or a mass of minerals filling up a crack where two rocks come together
4 An affectionate term for a domestic cat
5 Celebration
6 Loose or unmanned mine cart on the roll
7 Underground passage

Now, one thing that annoyed me when they brought us ponies out:
A bookie[8] looked at me, you know, and then began to shout,
"Two to one, bar one; I'll lay you ten to one!" you see?
While down the pit my "run" of tubs[9] is limited to three.
I thought, "What does he take me for? 'Ten to one I'll lay,' said he.
Here's another one will lay down too, if he puts ten tubs on me!"
My jockey then he mounted, we paraded down the course;
I seemed to hear the people shout, "My word! Ain't he some horse!"

We then went to the starting post, all feeling quite sublime,
Where some chap with a little flag formed us into a line.
My driver said, "You've got to win, so do not disappoint!"
I felt like asking him if he had changed his "Tommy Point."
At last, we're off—and scamper up the course by scores of coppers,[10]
"Oh, Lord!" I thought, "What's coming off? My driver's missed his lockers!"
He digs his heels into me, as on my back he's stooping,
And then I think, "What's up with him? Is he afraid of roofing?"

---

8 Someone who bets money on horse races
9 The number of carts being pulled, train-like, by a pony at one time
10 Policemen

Now as I galloped on and on, my driver seemed to say,
"Go on for all you're worth, because there's no muck down today!"
I made a special effort, my driver he sat tight,
But just two lengths ahead of me was a pony on my right.
We'd not much further now to go; I could see the winning post.
That pony still in front of me was what upset me most.
My driver let me have my head, then my best form I showed
As that pony seemed to stumble and get off of the road.

'Twas over now, I'd passed the post—the sun was shining bright.
I'd won! And those who backed me were frantic with delight.
So when you talk of "Donoghue," "Humorist," and "Square Measure,"
Please don't forget 'twas I who won the "Pit Pony St. Ledger."
I've had thirteen weeks holiday, I have, upon my soul,
And now I'm back down pit again, getting out some coal.
If ponies down pits could speak, with one accord they'd cry,
"If there could only be another strike, we'll let the rest of the world go by!"

Arthur Morris

My Dog

Have you seen a little dog anywhere about?
A raggy dog, a shaggy dog,
      who's always looking out
For some fresh mischief which he thinks
      he really ought to do.
He's very likely at this minute
      biting someone's shoe.

If you see that little dog,
      his tail up in the air,
A whirly tail, a curly tail,
      a dog who doesn't care
For any other dog he meets,
      not even for himself,
Then hide your mats, and put your meat
      upon the top-most shelf.

If you see that little dog, barking at the cars,
A raggy dog, a shaggy dog,
      with eyes like twinkling stars,
Just let me know, for though he's bad,
      as bad as bad can be,
I wouldn't change that dog for all
      the treasures of the sea.

Emily Lewis

My New Rabbit

We brought him home, I was so pleased,
    We made a rabbit-hutch,
I give him oats, I talk to him,
    I love him very much.

Now when I talk to Rover dog,
    He answers me "Bow-wow!"
And when I speak to Pussy-cat,
    She purrs and says "Mee-ow!"

But Bunny never says a word,
    Just twinkles with his nose,
And what that rabbit thinks about,
    Why! no one ever knows.

My Mother says the fairies must
    Have put on him a spell,
They told him all their secrets, then
    They whispered, "Pray don't tell."

So Bunny sits there looking wise,
    And twinkling with his nose,
And never, never, never tells
    A single thing he knows.

Elizabeth Gould

I Met a Rat of Culture

I met a rat of culture
who was elegantly dressed
in a pair of velvet trousers
and a silver-buttoned vest,
he related ancient proverbs
and recited poetry,
he spoke a dozen languages,
eleven more than me.

The rat was perspicacious,
and had cogent things to say
on bionics, economics,
hydroponics, and ballet,
he instructed me in sculpture,
he shed light on keeping bees,
then he painted an acrylic
of an abstract view of cheese.
He had circled the equator,
he had visited the poles,
he extolled the art of sailing
while he baked assorted rolls,
he wove a woolen carpet
and he shaped a porcelain pot,
then he sang an operetta
while he danced a slow gavotte.
He was versed in jet propulsion,
an authority on trains,

all of botany and baseball
were contained within his brains,
he knew chemistry and physics,
he had taught himself to sew,
to my knowledge, there was nothing
that the rodent did not know.

He was vastly more accomplished
than the billions of his kin,
he performed a brief sonata
on a tiny violin,
but he squealed and promptly vanished
at the entrance of my cat,
for despite his erudition,
he was nothing but a rat.

Jack Prelutsky

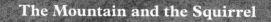

The Mountain and the Squirrel

The mountain and the squirrel
Had a quarrel,
And the former called the latter "Little Prig";
Bun replied,
"You are doubtless very big;
But all sorts of things and weather
Must be taken in together
To make up a year,
And a sphere.
And I think it no disgrace
To occupy my place.
If I'm not so large as you,
You are not so small as I,
And not half so spry.
I'll not deny you make
A very pretty squirrel track.
Talents differ; all is well and wisely put;
If I cannot carry forests on my back,
Neither can you crack a nut!"

Ralph Waldo Emerson

The Grasshopper and the Elephant

Way down south where bananas grow,
A grasshopper stepped on an elephant's
  toe.
The elephant said, with tears in his eyes,
"Pick on somebody your own size."

Anonymous

The Owl and the Pussy-Cat

The Owl and the Pussy-cat went to sea
In a beautiful pea-green boat,
They took some honey, and plenty of money,
Wrapped up in a five-pound note.
The Owl looked up to the stars above,
And sang to a small guitar,
"O lovely Pussy! O Pussy, my love,
What a beautiful Pussy you are,
You are,
You are!
What a beautiful Pussy you are!"

Pussy said to the Owl, "You elegant fowl!
How charmingly sweet you sing!
O let us be married! Too long we have tarried:
But what shall we do for a ring?"

They sailed away, for a year and a day,
To the land where the Bong-Tree grows,
And there in a wood a Piggy-wig stood,
With a ring at the end of his nose,
His nose,
His nose,
With a ring at the end of his nose.

"Dear Pig, are you willing to sell for one shilling your ring?"
Said the Piggy, "I will."
So they took it away, and were married next day
By the Turkey who lives on the hill.
They dined on mince, and slices of quince,
Which they ate with a runcible spoon;

And hand in hand, on the edge of the sand,
They danced by the light of the moon,
The moon,
The moon,
They danced by the light of the moon.

Edward Lear

Sea-Fever

Sea-Fever

The first two poems Emma and I thought of when we began this collection were "Sea-Fever" and "Cargoes" by John Masefield. They were the first poems I ever memorized as a child, and they're great read-alouds, for their imagery is so splendid.

If I'm ever asked to name my favorite song, "My Ship" is usually what first comes to mind (followed immediately by a host of others!), and I simply had to include Ira Gershwin's glorious words in this anthology.

We're a sea- and waterways-loving family. I grew up near the River Thames, which is probably why Tennyson's "The Brook" resonates with me. Brooks, riverlets, and streams abound in England and have always sparked my imagination.

We discovered Rachel Lyman Field's "If Once You Have Slept on an Island" as we were putting this book together, and it has become a new favorite. Having both been fortunate enough to spend vacations on several different islands, we agree this lovely poem says it all.

Both Emma and I have chosen to make our homes by the sea and are thankful that our spouses share our passion for it.

Both Emma and I have chosen to make our homes by the sea and are thankful that our spouses share our passion for it.

The smell of brine, the cry of seagulls, the *clang* of buoy bells and *ping* of lines slapping against ships' masts, the echo of a foghorn from a lighthouse as the sea mist rolls in, the feeling of sun-warmed sand between the toes and salty sea spray on the face and in the hair, the fun of finding the *perfect* keepsake among the shells and pebbles: These simple joys have given us countless happy memories.

—*J. A.*

Sea-Fever

I must go down to the seas again, to the lonely sea and the sky,
And all I ask is a tall ship and a star to steer her by,
And the wheel's kick and the wind's song and the white sail's shaking,
And a gray mist on the sea's face and a gray dawn breaking.

I must go down to the seas again, for the call of the running tide
Is a wild call and a clear call that may not be denied;
And all I ask is a windy day with the white clouds flying,
And the flung spray and the blown spume, and the sea-gulls crying.

I must go down to the seas again to the vagrant gypsy life.
To the gull's way and the whale's way where the wind's like a whetted knife;
And all I ask is a merry yarn from a laughing fellow-rover,
And quiet sleep and a sweet dream when the long trick's over.

John Masefield

I Started Early

I started Early—took my Dog—
And visited the Sea—
The Mermaids in the Basement
Came out to look at me—

And Frigates—in the Upper Floor
Extended Hempen Hands—
Presuming Me to be a Mouse—
Aground—upon the Sands—

But no Man moved Me—till the Tide
Went past my simple Shoe—
And past my Apron—and my Belt
And past my Bodice—too—

And made as He would eat me up—
As wholly as a Dew
Upon a Dandelion's Sleeve—
And then—I started—too—

And He—He followed—close behind—
I felt his Silver Heel
Upon my—Ankle—Then my Shoes
Would overflow with Pearl—

Until We met the Solid Town—
No One He seemed to know—
And bowing—with a Mighty look—
At me—The Sea withdrew—

Emily Dickinson

The Sea

The sea is a hungry dog,
Giant and grey.
He rolls on the beach all day.
With his clashing teeth and shaggy jaws
Hour upon hour he gnaws
The rumbling, tumbling stones,
And "Bones, bones, bones, bones!"
The giant sea-dog moans,
Licking his greasy paws.

And when the night wind roars
And the moon rocks in the stormy cloud,
He bounds to his feet and snuffs and sniffs,
Shaking his wet sides over the cliffs,
And howls and hollos long and loud.

But on quiet days in May and June,
When even the grasses on the dune
Play no more their reedy tune,
With his head between his paws
He lies on the sandy shores,
So quiet, so quiet, he scarcely snores.

James Reeves

Noticing

I was looking at the sea just now,
watching the swirling, white-foamed waves.
Four little birds flew across my vision
and I didn't know what they were called.

Is it enough
that I noticed them in the evening mist?
I see so many lovely things,
flowers, trees especially.
I would be proud to say
"that's a so-and-so, here's a—"
but I don't know.

I could learn.
And I did notice.
What makes me frown
is how much I missed while noting this down.

Julie Andrews

My Ship

My ship has sails that are made of silk,
The decks are trimmed with gold,
And of jam and spice there's a paradise in the hold.

My ship's aglow with a million pearls
And rubies fill each bin;
The sun sits high in a sapphire sky
When my ship comes in.

I can wait the years
'til it appears
One fine day, one spring.
But the pearls and such
They won't mean much
If there's missing just one thing.

I do not care if that day arrives
That dream need never be
If the ship I sing doesn't also bring
My own true love to me.

I can wait the years
'til it appears
One fine day, one spring.
But the pearls and such
They won't mean much
If there's missing just one thing.

I do not care if that day arrives
That dream need never be
If the ship I sing doesn't also bring
My own true love to me.

If the ship I sing doesn't also bring
My own true love to me.

Lyrics by Ira Gershwin
Music by Kurt Weill

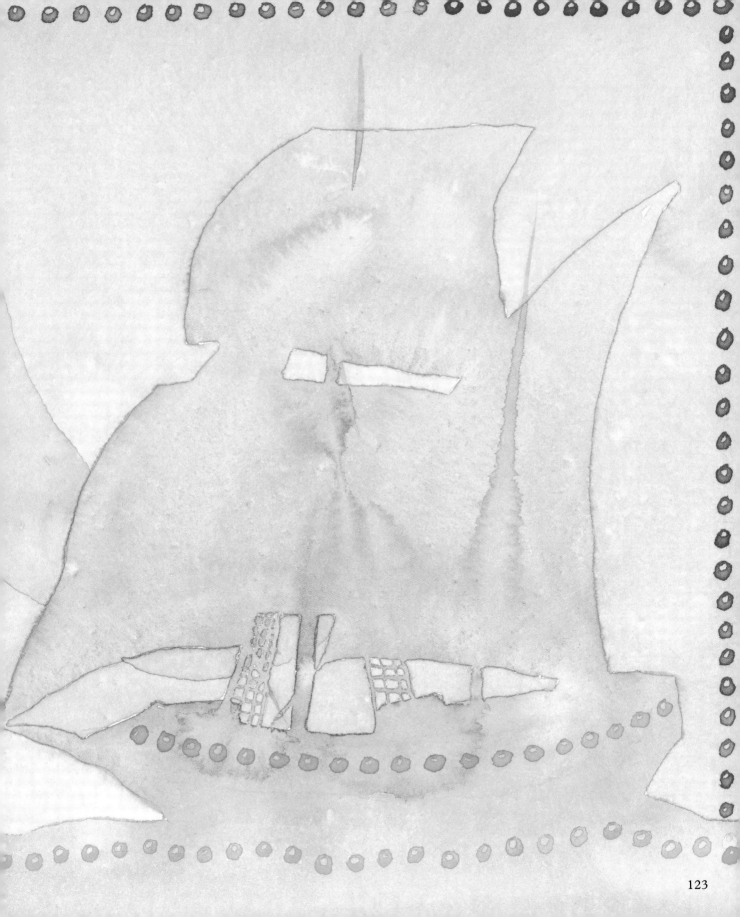

Cargoes

Quinquireme of Nineveh from distant Ophir,
Rowing home to haven in sunny Palestine,
With a cargo of ivory,
And apes and peacocks,
Sandalwood, cedarwood, and sweet white wine.

Stately Spanish galleon coming from the Isthmus,
Dipping through the Tropics by the palm-green shores,
With a cargo of diamonds,
Emeralds, amethysts,
Topazes, and cinnamon, and gold moidores.

Dirty British coaster with a salt-caked smoke stack,
Butting through the Channel in the mad March days,
With a cargo of Tyne coal,
Road-rails, pig-lead,
Firewood, iron-ware, and cheap tin trays.

John Masefield

I'd Like to Be a Lighthouse

I'd like to be a lighthouse
    All scrubbed and painted white.
I'd like to be a lighthouse
    And stay awake all night
To keep my eye on everything
    That sails my patch of sea;
I'd like to be a lighthouse
    With the ships all watching me.

Rachel Lyman Field

Mermaids

Leagues, leagues over
The sea I sail
Couched on a wallowing
Dolphin's tail:
The sky is on fire
The waves a-sheen;
I dabble my foot
In the billows green.

In a sea-weed hat
On the rocks I sit
Where tern and sea-mew
Glide and beat,
Where dark shadows
The cormorants meet.

In caverns cool
When the tide's a-wash,
I sound my conch
To the watery splash.

From out their grottoes
At evening's beam
The mermaids swim
With locks agleam.

To where I watch
On the yellow sands;
And they pluck sweet music
With sea-cold hands.

They bring me coral
And amber clear;
But when the stars
In heaven appear
Their music ceases,
They glide away,
And swim to their grottoes
Across the bay.

Then listen only
To my shrill tune,
The surfy tide,
And the wandering moon.

Walter de la Mare

126

If Once You Have Slept on an Island

If once you have slept on an island
   You'll never be quite the same;
You may look as you looked the day before
   And go by the same old name,

You may bustle about in street and shop;
   You may sit at home and sew,
But you'll see blue water and wheeling gulls
   Wherever your feet may go.

You may chat with the neighbors of this and that
   And close to your fire keep,
But you'll hear ship whistle and lighthouse bell
   And tides beat through your sleep.

Oh, you won't know why, and you can't say how
   Such change upon you came,
But—once you have slept on an island,
   You'll never be quite the same!

Rachel Lyman Field

Boats Sail on the Rivers

Boats sail on the rivers,
    And ships sail on the seas;
But clouds that sail across the sky
    Are prettier far than these.

There are bridges on the rivers,
    As pretty as you please;
But the bow that bridges heaven,
    And overtops the trees,
And builds a road from earth to sky,
    Is prettier far than these.

Christina Georgina Rossetti

What Are Heavy?

What are heavy? Sea-sand and sorrow;
What are brief? Today and tomorrow;
What are frail? Spring blossoms and youth;
What are deep? The ocean and truth.

Christina Georgina Rossetti

The Little Pebble's Song

They think he's silent. Me, I know he's singing,
singing beside the path his little pebble song.
But since he sings so softly, people really
have no idea . . .
Did he learn in the stream, or on the brooklet's dam,
the flowing waters' secrets? Or did he learn, along the
road, the secrets of creatures passing on their way?

Sabine Sicaud

The Brook

I come from haunts of coot and hern,
   I make a sudden sally,
And sparkle out among the fern,
   To bicker down a valley.

By thirty hills I hurry down,
   Or slip between the ridges,
By twenty thorpes, a little town,
   And half a hundred bridges.

Till last by Philip's farm I flow
   To join the brimming river,
For men may come and men may go,
   But I go on forever.

I chatter over stony ways,
   In little sharps and trebles,
I bubble into eddying bays,
   I babble on the pebbles.

With many a curve my banks I fret
   By many a field and fallow,
And many a fairy foreland set
   With willow-weed and mallow.

I chatter, chatter, as I flow
   To join the brimming river,
For men may come and men may go,
   But I go on forever.

I wind about, and in and out,
   With here a blossom sailing,
And here and there a lusty trout,
   And here and there a grayling,

And here and there a foamy flake
   Upon me, as I travel
With many a silvery waterbreak
   Above the golden gravel,

And draw them all along, and flow
   To join the brimming river,
For men may come and men may go,
   But I go on forever.

I steal by lawns and grassy plots,
   I slide by hazel covers;
I move the sweet forget-me-nots
   That grow for happy lovers.

I slip, I slide, I gloom, I glance,
   Among my skimming swallows;
I make the netted sunbeam dance
   Against my sandy shallows.

I murmur under moon and stars
   In brambly wildernesses;
I linger by my shingly bars,
   I loiter round my cresses;

And out again I curve and flow
   To join the brimming river,
For men may come and men may go,
   But I go on forever.

Alfred, Lord Tennyson

131

Laughing Song

Laughing Song

"The King's Breakfast" is the first poem I remember reading to Emma, and continues to be a favorite for us both. The idea of a king taking such simple pleasure in butter for his bread (and sliding down a banister when he gets it!) tickles our family funny bone.

We all share a rather wicked sense of humor—and I confess that poems like "Daddy Fell into the Pond" make me laugh outright. I can't get past the *title* of "The Turkey Shot out of the Oven" without being reduced to helpless giggles.

"My Auntie" is about a real town in Wales with the longest name in the world. We have a family member who is Welsh, and my grandkids grill him every time they see him — "Say that name again!" He has the patience of a saint, and we love him for his endless efforts to teach everyone to pronounce it. As the poem says, "it's hard to say"— and it *really* is! The Welsh have some of the sweetest singing voices in the world, but one must admit that their language is practically impossible for an outsider. There

We all share a rather wicked sense of humor

are a lot of sounds that seem to come from the back of the throat, rather like a cat clearing a hairball or Donald Duck with laryngitis…feel free, dear reader, to "hawk and gack" all you want while practicing the pronunciation we've attempted to provide!

—*J. A.*

Laughing Song

When the green woods laugh with the voice of joy,
And the dimpling stream runs laughing by;
When the air does laugh with our merry wit,
And the green hill laughs with the noise of it;

When the meadows laugh with lively green,
And the grasshopper laughs in the merry scene;
When Mary and Susan and Emily
With their sweet round mouths sing "Ha, ha, he!"

When the painted birds laugh in the shade,
Where our table with cherries and nuts is spread:
Come live, and be merry, and join with me,
To sing the sweet chorus of "Ha, ha, he!"

William Blake

Have You Ever Seen?

Have you ever seen a sheet on a river bed?
Or a single hair from a hammer's head?
Has the foot of a mountain any toes?
And is there a pair of garden hose?

Does the needle ever wink its eye?
Why doesn't the wing of a building fly?
Can you tickle the ribs of a parasol?
Or open the trunk of a tree at all?

Are the teeth of a rake ever going to bite?
Have the hands of a clock any left or right?
Can the garden plot be deep and dark?
And what is the sound of the birch's bark?

Anonymous

The Teapot and the Kettle

Said the teapot to the kettle,
"You are really in fine fettle,
You're a handsome piece of metal
Are you not, not, not?

"Your dimensions are so spacious,
And your waistline so capacious
And your whistle so flirtatious
When your water's hot."

Said the kettle, "Why you flatter
Me extremely, but no matter,
I have never seen a fatter
Teapot in my life.

"Though I would not call you dumpy,
You are round and sweet and plumpy
And I'm sure you're never grumpy.
Would you be my wife?"

Said the teapot to the kettle,
"Sir, my given name is Gretel
And I'd really like to settle
Down your wife to be."

So without the least delay
They were married the next day
And they both were very gay
Drinking tea, tea, tea.

Mary Ann Hoberman

137

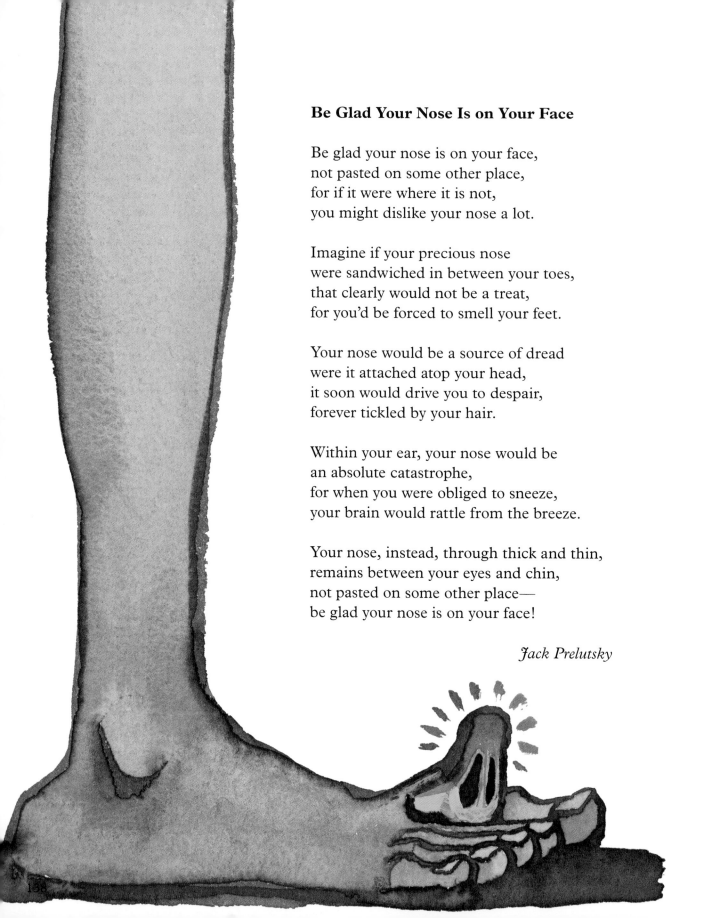

Be Glad Your Nose Is on Your Face

Be glad your nose is on your face,
not pasted on some other place,
for if it were where it is not,
you might dislike your nose a lot.

Imagine if your precious nose
were sandwiched in between your toes,
that clearly would not be a treat,
for you'd be forced to smell your feet.

Your nose would be a source of dread
were it attached atop your head,
it soon would drive you to despair,
forever tickled by your hair.

Within your ear, your nose would be
an absolute catastrophe,
for when you were obliged to sneeze,
your brain would rattle from the breeze.

Your nose, instead, through thick and thin,
remains between your eyes and chin,
not pasted on some other place—
be glad your nose is on your face!

Jack Prelutsky

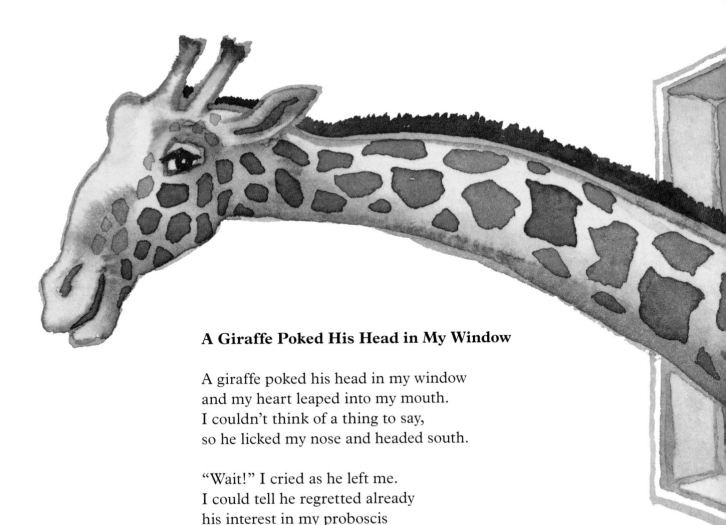

A Giraffe Poked His Head in My Window

A giraffe poked his head in my window
and my heart leaped into my mouth.
I couldn't think of a thing to say,
so he licked my nose and headed south.

"Wait!" I cried as he left me.
I could tell he regretted already
his interest in my proboscis
for his legs were extremely unsteady.

I thought, as I groped for my hanky
—and I pass this on to you—
that if a wild animal comes to call,
say a tiger, or meerkat, or 'roo . . .

If, like me, you want him to stay,
or even come back another day,
then perhaps it would really pay to say
"Welcome" and "How do you do"!

Julie Andrews

Bartholomew Blue

Bartholomew Blue was a gentleman who
Could never decide what he wanted to do.
Mornings began in a terrible way,
As he'd try to decide what to wear for the day.
Which trousers? What shirt? And which socks, and what shoes?
Bartholomew just wasn't able to choose.

Completely confounded, he'd settle once more
On what he had chosen the morning before.
He'd go down to breakfast (a little bit smelly),
And try to decide what to put in his belly.
Two fried eggs and bacon? Some cinnamon bread?
He'd end up with yesterday's oatmeal instead.

Each hour would bring yet another decision . . .
What program to watch on today's television?
What method of transport to travel to work?
Bartholomew worried he might go berserk!
And still he would choose what he'd chosen before,
Until life started seeming a terrible bore.

As time trickled by him, things didn't improve.
For the less he would try things, the less he would move.
His suit became smellier day after day
His shoelaces frayed and his socks turned to gray.
He longed for excitement—a fresh point of view.
But habit prevailed, and he chose what he knew.

Soon cobwebs began to appear here and there.
And one day, a bird built a nest in his hair.
Before poor Bartholomew knew what to do,
Another bird parked on his head, and then two!
Cardinals, blue jays and sparrows galore—
Followed by chickadees, finches and more.

Bartholomew stood there, stuck fast in his boots,
And before very long, he began to grow roots.
Then—just as the birds on his head had assumed,
He sprouted with branches and leaves, and he *bloomed*!
Bartholomew Blue is a tree to this day . . .
But at least now he gives off a fragrant bouquet.

Emma Walton Hamilton

Daddy Fell into the Pond

Everyone grumbled. The sky was grey.
We had nothing to do and nothing to say.
We were nearing the end of a dismal day,
And there seemed to be nothing beyond, THEN
    Daddy fell into the pond!

And everyone's face grew merry and bright,
And Timothy danced for sheer delight.
"Give me the camera, quick, oh quick!
He's crawling out of the duckweed." *Click!*

Then the gardener suddenly slapped his knee,
And doubled up, shaking silently,
And the ducks all quacked as if they were daft
And it sounded as if the old drake laughed.

O, there wasn't a thing that didn't respond WHEN
    Daddy fell into the pond!

Alfred Noyes

Missing

I've lost my sense of humor,
It fell into a well
That's full of dark self-pity,
As far as I can tell.

I'm glared at by the children.
I'm yelled at by the boss.
And every little word I say
Makes everybody cross.

I'd run away and not come back
If it would do some good.
But nobody would notice
So I don't think I should.

I miss my sense of humor
And if, by chance, you see
It peeking round a corner
Please send it back to me.

Julie Andrews

The ABC

'Twas midnight in the schoolroom
And every desk was shut
When suddenly from the alphabet
Was heard a loud "Tut-Tut!"

Said A to B, "I don't like C;
His manners are a lack.
For all I ever see of C
Is a semi-circular back!"

"I disagree," said D to B,
"I've never found C so.
From where I stand he seems to be
An uncompleted O."

C was vexed, "I'm much perplexed,
You criticize my shape.
I'm made like that, to help spell Cat
And Cow and Cool and Cape."

"He's right" said E; said F, "Whoopee!"
Said G, "'Ip, 'Ip, 'ooray!"
"You're dropping me," roared H to G.
"Don't do it please I pray."

"Out of my way," LL said to K.
"I'll make poor I look ILL."
To stop this stunt J stood in front,
And presto! ILL was JILL.

"U know," said V, "that W
Is twice the age of me.
For as a Roman V is five
I'm half as young as he."

X and Y yawned sleepily,
"Look at the time!" they said.
"Let's all get off to beddy byes."
They did, then "Z-z-z."

Spike Milligan

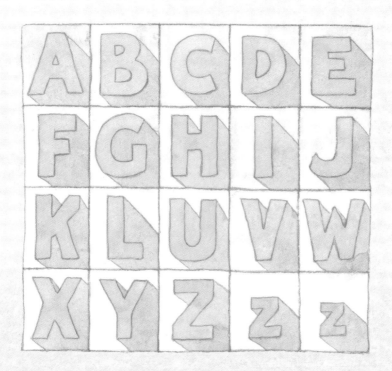

Today I'm Going Yesterday

Today I'm going yesterday
as quickly as I can,
I'm confident I'll do it,
I've devised a clever plan,
it involves my running backward
at a constant rate of speed,
if I'm mindful of my timing,
I'll undoubtedly succeed.

Today I'm going yesterday,
I'm moving very fast
as I'm putting off the future
for the rather recent past,
I can feel the present fading
as I hastily depart,
and look forward to arriving
on the day before I start.

Today I'm going yesterday,
I'm slipping out of sight
and anticipate I'll vanish
just a bit before tonight,
when I reach my destination,
I'll compose a note to say
that I'll see you all tomorrow,
which of course will be today.

Jack Prelutsky

145

The King's Breakfast

The King asked the Queen,
And the Queen asked the Dairymaid:
"Could we have some butter for the Royal slice of bread?"
The Queen asked the Dairymaid,
The Dairymaid said, "Certainly,
I'll go and tell the cow now
Before she goes to bed."

The Dairymaid she curtsied,
And went and told the Alderney:
"Don't forget the butter for the Royal slice of bread."
The Alderney said sleepily:
"You'd better tell His Majesty
That many people nowadays
Like marmalade instead."

The Dairymaid said, "Fancy!"
And went to Her Majesty.
She curtsied to the Queen, and she turned a little red:
"Excuse me, Your Majesty,
For taking of the liberty,
But marmalade is tasty,
If it's very thickly spread."

The Queen said "Oh!"
And went to His Majesty:
"Talking of the butter for the Royal slice of bread,
Many people think
That marmalade is nicer.
Would you like to try
A little marmalade instead?"

The King said, "Bother!"
And then he said, "Oh, dear me!"
The King sobbed, "Oh, deary me!"
And went back to bed.
"Nobody," he whimpered,
"Could call me a fussy man;
I *only* want a little bit of butter for my bread!"

The Queen said, "There, there!"
And went to the Dairymaid.
The Dairymaid said, "There, there!"
And went to the shed.
The cow said, "There, there!
I didn't really mean it;
Here's milk for his porringer,
And butter for his bread."

The Queen took the butter
And brought it to His Majesty;
The King said, "Butter, eh?"
And bounced out of bed.
"Nobody," he said,
as he kissed her tenderly,
"Nobody," he said,
as he slid down the banisters,
"Nobody, my darling,
Could call me a fussy man—
BUT
I do like a little bit of butter to my bread!"

A. A. Milne

My Auntie

My auntie who lives in
Llanfairpwllgwyngyllgogerych-
   wyrndrobwllllantysiliogogogoch*
Has asked me to stay.

But unfortunately
Llanfairpwllgwyngyllgogerych-
   wyrndrobwllllantysiliogogogoch
Is a long, long way away.

Will I ever go to
Llanfairpwllgwyngyllgogerych-
   wyrndrobwllllantysiliogogogoch?
It's difficult to say.

Colin West

* pronounced, roughly: "Clan-vire-pookh-guin-
gekh-go-ger-okh-queen-drob-okh-clantus-silio-
gogo-gokh," is the real name of a town in Wales
and means "the church of St. Mary in the hollow
of the white hazel near the fierce whirlpool and
the church of Tysilio by the red cave" in Welsh

Two Limericks

A lady named Marjorie Reed
Swallowed oysters whenever she'd feed.
She was hoping, poor girl,
To deliver a pearl—
But the best she produced was a bead.

★ ★ ★

A lady who smelled like a quince
Decided she'd have a good rinse.
She rubbed in great reams
Of rare vanishing creams
And hasn't been seen again since.

Tony Walton

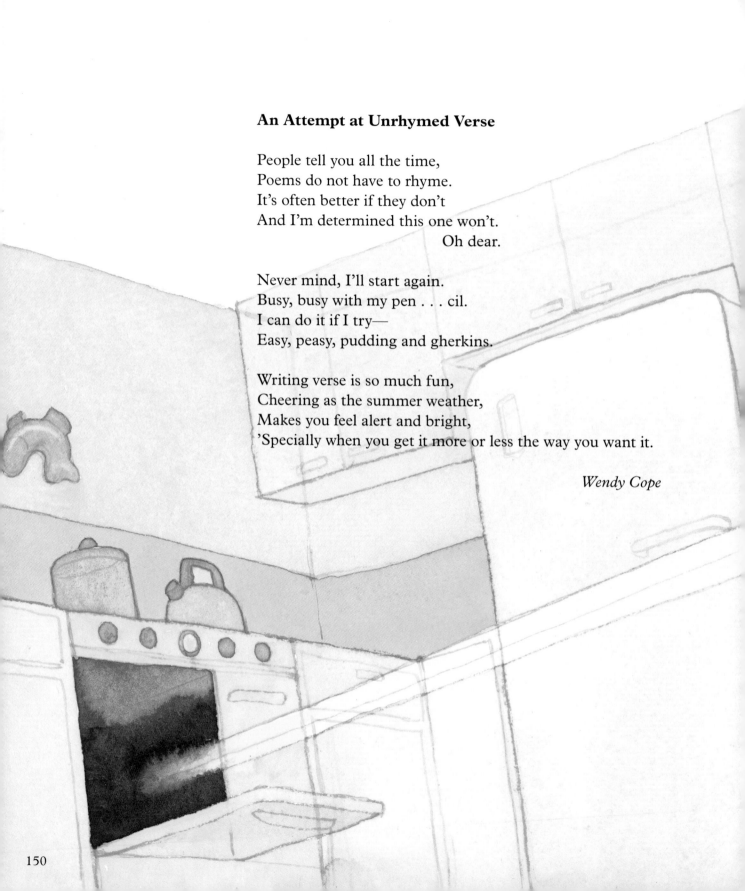

An Attempt at Unrhymed Verse

People tell you all the time,
Poems do not have to rhyme.
It's often better if they don't
And I'm determined this one won't.
                              Oh dear.

Never mind, I'll start again.
Busy, busy with my pen . . . cil.
I can do it if I try—
Easy, peasy, pudding and gherkins.

Writing verse is so much fun,
Cheering as the summer weather,
Makes you feel alert and bright,
'Specially when you get it more or less the way you want it.

Wendy Cope

The Turkey Shot Out of the Oven

The turkey shot out of the oven
and rocketed into the air,
it knocked every plate off the table
and partly demolished a chair.

It ricocheted into a corner
and burst with a deafening boom,
then splattered all over the kitchen,
completely obscuring the room.

It stuck to the walls and the windows,
it totally coated the floor,
there was turkey attached to the ceiling,
where there'd never been turkey before.

It blanketed every appliance,
it smeared every saucer and bowl,
there wasn't a way I could stop it,
that turkey was out of control.

I scraped and I scrubbed with displeasure,
and thought with chagrin as I mopped,
that I'd never again stuff a turkey
with popcorn that hadn't been popped.

Jack Prelutsky

151

Leisure

Leisure

"Leisure" is a rather sophisticated word, but its meaning is wonderful: free time, playtime. If you speak with an English accent, as I do, "leisure" rhymes with "pleasure"!

Have you ever looked at a painting and, when you stepped away, felt you could see the world *exactly* as the artist depicted it? Stephen Sondheim's beautiful song "Sunday" is about a famous painting called *A Sunday on La Grand Jatte* by Georges Seurat. The wonder of Sondheim's lyric is that he makes us see with his words what Seurat tried to do with his paintbrush. If you look at the painting closely, you realize that the park, the water, the trees, and even the people are actually made up of tiny flecks of paint — "color and light."

Emma and I love stories and poems that invite readers to notice the world in a different way. "Wind Pictures" does just that. We often play "the cloud game" with our families and are always delighted when we each see something different in the same cloud.

My little brother Chris used to sing "The Leader of the

Band" at my auntie's dancing school. At the age of five or six he performed it so enchantingly and received such an ovation that it quite turned his head. He became so impossibly full of himself that my mother never enrolled him in any further shows. Poor Chris—he was as starry-eyed about the theater as I am to this day. Read Rachel

Emma and I love stories and poems that invite readers to notice the world in a different way.

Lyman Field's "At the Theater" and you will feel the magic for yourself.

Actually, when you think about it, this section is not so much about leisure (English pronunciation!) as it is about pleasure—for whether we choose to read, write, paint, sing, or simply gaze at the stars, playtime nourishes the imagination and enriches life beyond measure.

—*J. A.*

Leisure

What is this life, if, full of care,
We have no time to stand and stare.

No time to stand beneath the boughs
And stare as long as sheep or cows.

No time to see, when woods we pass,
Where squirrels hide their nuts in grass.

No time to see, in broad daylight,
Streams full of stars, like skies at night.

No time to turn at Beauty's glance,
And watch her feet, how they can dance.

No time to wait till her mouth can
Enrich that smile her eyes began.

A poor life this, if, full of care,
We have no time to stand and stare.

W. H. Davies

Sunday

Sunday,
By the blue
Purple yellow red water
On the green
Purple yellow red grass,
Let us pass
Through our perfect park,
Pausing on a Sunday
By the cool
Blue triangular water
On the soft
Green elliptical grass
As we pass
Through arrangements of shadows
Towards the verticals of trees
Forever . . .

By the blue
Purple yellow red water
On the green
Orange violet mass
Of the grass
In our perfect park

Made of flecks of light
And dark,
And parasols:
Bumbum bum bumbumbum
Bumbum bum . . .

People strolling through the trees
Of a small suburban park
On an island in the river
On an ordinary Sunday . . .

Lyrics and music by
Stephen Sondheim

Afternoon on a Hill

I will be the gladdest thing
    Under the sun!
I will touch a hundred flowers
    And not pick one.

I will look at cliffs and clouds
    With quiet eyes,
Watch the wind bow down the grass,
    And the grass rise.

And when the lights begin to show
    Up from the town,
I will mark which must be mine,
    And then start down!

Edna St. Vincent Millay

Wind Pictures

Look! There's a giant stretching in the sky,
A thousand white-maned horses flying by,
A house, a mother mountain with her hills,
A lazy lady posing in her frills,
Cotton floating from a thousand bales,
And a white ship with white sails.

See the old witch fumbling with her shawl,
White towers piling on a castle wall,
The bits of soft that break and fall away,
Air-borne mushrooms with undersides of gray—
Above, a white doe races with her fawn
On the white grass of a celestial lawn.
Lift up your lovely heads and look
As wind turns clouds into a picture book.

Mary O'Neill

The Ice-Cream Man

When summer's in the city,
    And brick's a blaze of heat,
The Ice-Cream Man with his little cart
    Goes trundling down the street.

Beneath his round umbrella,
    Oh, what a joyful sight,
To see him fill the cones with mounds
    Of cooling brown or white;

Vanilla, chocolate, strawberry,
    Or chilly things to drink
From bottles full of frosty-fizz,
    Green, orange, white, or pink.

His cart might be a flower bed
    Of roses and sweet peas,
The way the children cluster round
    As thick as honeybees.

Rachel Lyman Field

A Book

There is no Frigate like a Book
To take us Lands away
Nor any Coursers like a Page
Of prancing Poetry—
This Traverse may the poorest take
Without oppress of toll—
How frugal is the Chariot
That bears the Human soul.

Emily Dickinson

At the Library

I flip the pages of a book and slip inside,
where crystal seas await and pirates hide.
I find a paradise where birds can talk,
where children fly and trees prefer to walk.
Sometimes I end up on a city street.
I recognize the brownskin girl I meet.
She's skinny, but she's strong, and brave, and wise.
I smile, because I see *me* in her eyes.

Nikki Grimes

Oh, For a Book

Oh, for a book and a shady nook,
   Either in door or out;
With the green leaves whisp'ring
   overhead or the street cries all about.
Where I may read all at my ease,
   both of the new and old;
For a jolly good book whereon to
   look is better to me than gold.

Christopher North

Keep a Poem in Your Pocket

Keep a poem in your pocket
and a picture in your head
and you'll never feel lonely
at night when you're in bed.

The little poem will sing to you
the little picture bring to you
a dozen dreams to dance to you
at night when you're in bed.

So—
Keep a picture in your pocket
and a poem in your head
and you'll never feel lonely
at night when you're in bed.

Beatrice Schenk de Regniers

What's a Poem?

A whisper, a shout, thoughts turned inside out.
A laugh, a sigh, an echo passing by.
A rhythm, a rhyme, a moment caught in time.
A moon, a star, a glimpse of who you are.

Charles Ghigna

The Reading Mother

You may have tangible wealth untold:
Caskets of jewels and coffers of gold.
Richer than I you can never be—
I had a Mother who read to me.

Strickland Gillilan
(Abridged version)

When Mother Reads Aloud

When mother reads aloud, the past
Seems real as every day;
I hear the tramp of armies vast,
I see the spears and lances cast,
I join the thrilling fray;
Brave knights and ladies fair and proud
I meet when mother reads aloud.

When mother reads aloud, far lands
Seem very near and true;
I cross the deserts' gleaming sands,
Or hunt the jungle's prowling bands,
Or sail the ocean blue;
Far heights, whose peaks the cold mists shroud,
I scale, when mother reads aloud.

When mother reads aloud, I long
For noble deeds to do—
To help the right, redress the wrong,
It seems so easy to be strong, so
    simple to be true.
O, thick and fast the visions crowd
My eyes, when mother reads aloud.

Anonymous

Picture Books in Winter

Summer fading, winter comes—
Frosty mornings, tingling thumbs,
Window robins, winter rooks,
And the picture story-books.

Water now is turned to stone
Nurse and I can walk upon;
Still we find the flowing brooks
In the picture story-books.

All the pretty things put by,
Wait upon the children's eye,
Sheep and shepherds, trees and crooks,
In the picture story-books.

We may see how all things are
Seas and cities, near and far,
And the flying fairies' looks,
In the picture story-books.

How am I to sing your praise,
Happy chimney-corner days,
Sitting safe in nursery nooks,
Reading picture story-books?

Robert Louis Stevenson

Paint Box

"Cobalt and umber and ultramarine,
Ivory, black and emerald green—
What shall I paint to give pleasure to you?"
"Paint for me somebody utterly new."

"I have painted you tigers in crimson and white."
"The colors were good and you painted aright."
"I have painted the cook and a camel in blue
And a panther in purple." "You painted them true.

"Now mix me a color that nobody knows,
And paint me a country where nobody goes.
And put in it people a little like you,
Watching a unicorn drinking the dew."

Emile Victor Rieu

Singing Time

I wake in the morning early
And always, the very first thing,
I poke out my head and I sit up in bed
And I sing and I sing and I sing.

Rose Fyleman

I'm the Leader of the Band

I'm the leader of the band
You should see me on parade
With a glove on either hand
Uniform with yards of braid
When we're playing in the park
Girls cry "Isn't music grand?!"
But there's not a doubt they all mean ME
'Cause I'm the leader of the big brass band.

Anonymous

The Floral Dance

As I walked home on a summer night
When stars in the heaven were shining bright
Far away from the footlight's glare
Into the sweet and scented air
Of a quaint old Cornish town

Borne from afar on the gentle breeze
Joining the murmur of summer seas
Distant tones of an old world dance
Played by the village band perchance
On the calm air came floating down

I thought I could hear the curious tone
Of the cornet, clarinet, and big trombone
Fiddle, cello, big bass drum,
Bassoon, flute, and euphonium
Far away, as in a trance
I heard the sound of the Floral Dance

And soon I heard such a bustling and prancing
And then I saw the whole village was dancing
In and out of the houses they came
Old folk, young folk, all the same
In that quaint old Cornish town

Every boy took a girl 'round the waist
And hurried her off in tremendous haste
Whether they knew one another I care not
Whether they cared at all, I know not
But they kissed as they danced along

And there was the band with that curious tone
Of the cornet, clarinet, and big trombone
Fiddle, cello, big bass drum,
Bassoon, flute, and euphonium
Each one making the most of his chance
All together in the Floral Dance

I felt so lonely standing there
And I could only stand and stare
For I had no boy with me
Lonely I should have to be
In that quaint old Cornish town

When suddenly hastening down the lane
A figure I knew I saw quite plain
With outstretched hands he came along
And carried me into that merry throng
And fiddle and all went dancing down

We danced to the band with the curious tone
Of the cornet, clarinet, and big trombone
Fiddle, cello, big bass drum,
Bassoon, flute, and euphonium
Each one making the most of his chance
All together in the Floral Dance

Dancing here, prancing there
Jigging, jogging everywhere
Up and down, and 'round the town
Hurrah! For the Floral Dance

Lyrics and music by Katie Moss

At the Theater

The sun was bright when we went in,
  But night and lights were there,
The walls had golden trimming on
  And plush on every chair.

The people talked; the music played,
  Then it grew black as pitch,
Yes, black as closets full of clothes,
  Or caves, I don't know which.

The curtain rolled itself away,
  It went I don't know where,
But, oh, that country just beyond,
  I do wish we lived there!

The mountain peaks more jagged rise,
  Grass grows more green than here;
The people there have redder cheeks,
  And clothes more gay and queer.

They laugh and smile, but not the same,
  Exactly as we do,
And if they ever have to cry
  Their tears are different, too—

More shiny, somehow, and more sad,
  You hold your breath to see
If everything will come out right
  And they'll live happily;

If Pierrot will kiss Pierrette
  Beneath an orange moon,
And Harlequin and Columbine
  Outwit old Pantaloon.

You know they will, they always do,
  But still your heart must beat,
And you must pray they will be saved,
  And tremble in your seat.

And then it's over and they bow
  All edged about with light,
The curtain rattles down and shuts
  Them everyone from sight.

It's strange to find the afternoon
  Still bright outside the door,
And all the people hurrying by
  The way they were before!

Rachel Lyman Field

The Wonderful World

The Wonderful World

Imagine for a moment that you are an astronaut, standing on the moon and looking back at the earth. All the "favorite things" we've explored in this book — trees, animals, children, laughter, the ocean, the arts — are contained in this one wondrous, blue-green jewel of a planet.

How important it is that we take care of it!

We might start by appreciating the majesty and beauty that is under our very noses, and let it "speak to us" as Chief Dan George does in his wonderful poem. We should protect and preserve nature and our environment, as Myra Cohn Livingston counsels in "Prayer for the Earth." And we can unite as people, celebrating our differences as well as our similarities.

The beautiful song "Nature Boy," by eden ahbez, will, I think, endure for generations to come, for its message is timeless — that we must love ourselves, our neighbor, and our fragile, diverse, magnificent world.

We must love ourselves, our neighbor,
and our fragile, diverse,
magnificent world.

Finally, we can ask ourselves what our unique contribution to it might be. John Bucchino's "Gift"—the final song in the stage adaptation of Emma's and my book, *Simeon's Gift* — seems the perfect choice to end this book. I hope you love the last line as much as I do, and that you will hold the words close to your heart.

—J. A.

The Wonderful World

Great, wide, beautiful, wonderful world,
With the wonderful water round you curled,
And the wonderful grass upon your breast,
World, you are beautifully drest.

The wonderful air is over me,
And the wonderful wind is shaking the tree—
It walks on the water, and whirls the mills,
And talks to itself on top of the hills.

You friendly Earth, how far do you go,
With the wheat-fields that nod and the rivers that flow
With cities and gardens, and cliffs, and isles,
And people upon you for thousands of miles?

Ah! you are so great, and I am so small,
I hardly can think of you, World, at all;
And yet, when I said my prayers to-day,
My mother kissed me, and said, quite gay,

"If the wonderful World is great to you,
And great to father and mother, too,

You are more than the Earth, though you are such a dot!
You can love and think, and the Earth cannot!"

William Brighty Rands

The Toys Talk of the World

"I should like," said the vase from the china-store,
"To have seen the world a little more.

"When they carried me here I was wrapped up tight,
But they say it is really a lovely sight."

"Yes," said a little plaster bird,
"That is exactly what *I* have heard;

"There are thousands of trees, and oh, what a sight
It must be when the candles are all alight."

The fat top rolled on his other side:
"It's not in the least like that," he cried.

"Except myself and the kite and the ball,
None of you know the world at all.

"There are houses and pavements hard and red,
And everything spins around," he said;

"Sometimes it goes slowly, and sometimes fast,
And often it stops with a bump at last."

The wooden donkey nodded his head:
"I had heard the world was like that," he said.

The kite and the ball exchanged a smile,
But they did not speak; it was not worth while.

Katharine Pyle

177

A Nation's Strength

Not gold, but only men can make
   A people great and strong;
Men who, for truth and honor's sake,
   Stand fast and suffer long.

Brave men who work while others sleep,
   Who dare while others fly—
They build a nation's pillars deep
   And lift them to the sky.

Ralph Waldo Emerson
(Abridged version)

Colors

My skin is kind of sort of brownish
Pinkish yellowish white.
My eyes are greyish blueish-green
But I'm told they look orange in the night.
My hair is reddish blondish brown,
But it's silver when it's wet.
And all the colors I am inside
Have not been invented yet.

Shel Silverstein

People

Some people talk and talk
and never say a thing.
Some people look at you
and birds begin to sing.

Some people laugh and laugh
and yet you want to cry.
Some people touch your hand
and music fills the sky.

Charlotte Zolotow

Skyscrapers

Do skyscrapers ever grow tired
   Of holding themselves up high?
Do they ever shiver on frosty nights
   With their tops against the sky?
Do they feel lonely sometimes
   Because they have grown so tall?
Do they ever wish they could lie right down
   And never get up at all?

Rachel Lyman Field

New York City

Yellow daffodils in town.
Bitter lemons. Buttercups.
From my tower I'll descend
To walk three blocks and meet a friend.
Along the asphalt I will go
And watch the New York taxis flow.

Julie Andrews

City

In the morning the city
Spreads its wings
Making a song
In stone that sings.

In the evening the city
Goes to bed
Hanging lights
About its head.

Langston Hughes

Breaks Free

I just want to be
where the earth breaks free
of concrete and metal and glass,
of asphalt and plastic and gas,
where sun is king
and water is queen,
where cactus grow tall
and the air is clean.
I just want to be
where the earth breaks free
of fences and alleys and walls,
of factories and traffic and malls,
where owls sleep
in the heart of day
waiting for sunset
to hunt their prey,
where mountains rise
in seas of sand
and coyotes roam
across the land.

Frank Asch

Landscape

What will you find at the edge of the world?
A footprint,
a feather,
desert sand swirled?
A tree of ice,
a rain of stars,
or a junkyard of cars?

What will there be at the rim of the earth?
A mollusk,
a mammal,
a new creature's birth?
Eternal sunrise,
immortal sleep,
or cars piled up in a rusty heap?

Eve Merriam

Prayer for Earth

Last night
an owl
called from the hill.
Coyotes howled.
A deer stood still
nibbling at bushes far away.
The moon shone silver.
Let this stay.

Today
two noisy crows
flew by,
their shadows pasted to the sky.
The sun broke out
through clouds of gray.
An iris opened.
Let this stay.

Myra Cohn Livingston

High Flight

Oh, I have slipped the surly bonds of earth,
And danced the skies on laughter-silvered wings;
Sunward I've climbed and joined the tumbling mirth
Of sun-split clouds—and done a hundred things
You have not dreamed of—wheeled and soared and swung
High in the sunlit silence. Hovering there
I've chased the shouting wind along and flung
My eager craft through footless halls of air.
Up, up the long delirious burning blue,
I've topped the windswept heights with easy grace
Where never lark, or even eagle, flew;
And, while with silent, lifting mind I've trod
The high untrespassed sanctity of space,
Put out my hand, and touched the face of God.

John Gillespie Magee Jr.

Dreams

Beyond, beyond the mountain line,
　The grey-stone and the boulder,
Beyond the growth of dark green pine,
　That crowns its western shoulder,
There lies that fairy land of mine,
　Unseen of a beholder.

Its fruits are all like rubies rare,
　Its streams are clear as glasses;
There golden castles hang in air,
　And purple grapes in masses,
And noble knights and ladies fair
　Come riding down the passes.

Ah me! they say if I could stand
　Upon those mountain ledges,
I should but see on either hand
　Plain fields and dusty hedges:
And yet I know my fairy land
　Lies somewhere o'er their edges.

Cecil Frances Alexander

Untitled

The beauty of the trees,
the softness of the air,
the fragrance of the grass,
　speaks to me.

The summit of the mountain,
the thunder of the sky,
the rhythm of the sea,
　speaks to me.

The faintness of the stars,
the freshness of the morning,
the dewdrop on the flower,
　speaks to me.

The strength of the fire,
the taste of salmon,
the trail of the sun,
and the life that never goes away,
　they speak to me.

And my heart soars.

Chief Dan George

My Symphony

To live content with small means,
to seek elegance rather than luxury,
and refinement rather than fashion,
to be worthy, not respectable, and wealthy, not rich,
to study hard, think quietly, talk gently, act frankly,
to listen to stars and birds, babes and sages, with open heart,
to bear all cheerfully,
do all bravely,
await occasions,
hurry never—
in a word, to let the spiritual, unbidden and unconscious,
grow up through the common.
This is to be my symphony.

William Ellery Channing

Nature Boy

There was a boy . . .
A very strange enchanted boy
They say he wandered very far, very far
Over land and sea
A little shy and sad of eye
But very wise was he
And then one day
One magic day he passed my way
And while we spoke of many things
Fools and kings
This he said to me
The greatest thing you'll ever learn
Is just to love and be loved in return

Lyrics and music by eden ahbez

Gift

Travel the world and you'll surely come to see
Ev'rything there is a part of you and me
Never let doubt put you in a spin
Ev'rything out is a part of in
Ev'rything wants you complete as you can be

We each are meant to share our song
You'll find it sang within you all along
Small but strong

Imagine that world stretching far and wide
Needing that song that you hold inside
Needing your gift to complete a grand design
Offer your gift to the world
And watch it shine!

Lyrics by John Bucchino
Music by Ian Fraser
From Simeon's Gift

ACKNOWLEDGMENTS

eden ahbez: "Nature Boy," reprinted with the permission of Golden World.

Howard Alexander and Billy Mayerl: "These Precious Things," copyright © 1948 by WB Music Corp, copyright renewed, all rights reserved worldwide.

Frank Asch: "Breaks Free," from *Cactus Poems*, copyright © 1998 by Frank Asch, reprinted by permission of Houghton Mifflin Harcourt Publishing Company.

Cicely Mary Barker: "The Song of the Beech Tree Fairy" from *Flower Fairies: The Little Green Book*, copyright © 1926, 1940, 1948 by the Estate of Cicely Mary Barker, reprinted by permission.

Harry Behn: "Trees" from *The Little Hill*, copyright © 1949 by Harry Behn, renewed 1977 by Alice L. Behn, reprinted by permission of Marian Reiner.

Alan and Marilyn Bergman: "And I'll Be There" (Threesome Music/Roaring Folk Music, music by Dave Grusin), reprinted by permission, all rights reserved.

Leslie Bricusse: "Talk to the Animals" from *Doctor Doolittle*, copyright © 1967 EMI Hastings Catalog, Inc., all rights controlled by EMI Hastings Catalog, Inc. (Publishing) and Alfred Publishing Co., Inc. (Print), all rights reserved.

John Bucchino and Ian Fraser: "Gift," copyright © 2006 by John Bucchino, Art Food Music owner of publication and allied rights throughout the world (administered by Williamson Music), international copyright secured, all rights reserved, reprinted by permission.

Marchette Chute: "Spring Rain" from *Around and About: Rhymes*, copyright © 1957 by E. P. Dutton, renewed 1985 by Marchette Chute, reprinted by permission of Elizabeth Hauser.

Wendy Cope: "An Attempt at Unrhymed Verse" from *Two Cures for Love: Selected Poems 1979–2006*, copyright © 2008 by Wendy Cope, reprinted by permission of Faber & Faber, Ltd. and PFD, Ltd. (www.pfd.co.uk) on behalf of Wendy Cope; "The Orange" from *Serious Concerns*, copyright © 1992 by Wendy Cope, reprinted by permission of Faber & Faber, Ltd. and PFD, Ltd. on behalf of the author.

Walter de la Mare: "Mermaid" from *The Complete Poems of Walter de la Mare* (1975 reprint), reprinted by permission of The Literary Trustees of Walter de la Mare and The Society of Authors as their representative; "Nicholas Nye" from *The Complete Poems of Walter de la Mare* (1975 reprint), reprinted by permission of The Literary Trustees of Walter de la Mare and The Society of Authors as their representative.

Rachel Field: "At the Theatre" from *Taxis and Toadstools: Verses and Decorations*, copyright ©1926 by Doubleday, reprinted by permission of Random House Children's Books, a division of Random House, Inc.; "I'd Like to Be a Lighthouse" from *Taxis and Toadstools: Verses and Decorations*, copyright © 1926 by Doubleday, reprinted by permission of Random House Children's Books, a division of Random House, Inc.; "The Ice-Cream Man" from *Taxis and Toadstools: Verses and Decorations*, copyright © 1926 by Doubleday, reprinted by permission of Random House Children's Books, a division of Random House, Inc.; "If Once You Have Slept on an Island" from *Taxis and Toadstools: Verses and Decorations*, copyright © 1926 by Doubleday, reprinted by permission of Random House Children's Books, a division of Random House, Inc.; "Skyscrapers" from *Poems*, copyright © 1957 by Macmillan Publishing Company, renewed 1985 by Arthur S. Pederson, reprinted by permission of Atheneum Books for Young Readers, an imprint of Simon & Schuster Children's Publishing Division; "Something Told the Wild Geese" from *Poems*, copyright © 1957 by Macmillan Publishing Company, renewed 1985 by Arthur S. Pederson, reprinted by permission of Atheneum Books for Young Readers, an imprint of Simon & Schuster Children's Publishing Division, recorded by permission of the Vice President of Estates of Special Investments, Harvard University.

For our family—and families everywhere.
—J. A. & E. W. H.

To Leigh and Andrew and to all my terrific models,
Paulo, Alex, Ruby, Hayden, Leah, and Griffin.
—J. M.

Little, Brown Books for Young Readers

Hachette Book Group
237 Park Avenue, New York, NY 10017
Visit our Web site at www.lb-kids.com

Little, Brown Books for Young Readers is a division of Hachette Book Group, Inc.
The Little, Brown name and logo are trademarks of Hachette Book Group, Inc.

First Edition: October 2009

Library of Congress Cataloging-in-Publication Data

Julie Andrews' collection of poems, songs, and lullabies / edited by Julie Andrews
and Emma Walton Hamilton; paintings by James McMullan.—1st ed.
      p. cm.
   ISBN 978-0-316-04049-5
1. Children's poetry. 2. Lullabies. I. Edwards, Julie, 1935–
II. Hamilton, Emma Walton. III. McMullan, James, 1934– ill.
   PN6109.97.J85 2009
   808.81'0083—dc22
                        2009005121

10 9 8 7 6 5 4 3 2 1
IM
Printed in Spain

The illustrations for this book were done in watercolor.
The text was set in Plantin, and the display type is Bickham Script Pro.
Book design by Patti Ann Harris